"*I never expected to see you again!*"

"I know that, tiger-eyes. I was shocked, too. But not so shocked that I didn't recognize it wasn't horror in your eyes when you looked at me, but hunger!"

Reba had hungered—for the love she felt only with him! Hunter had only seen the wanting as sexual!

"So Cousin Eliot's the sucker you've got your hooks into. Does he know you're only marrying him for his money?"

AMANDA BROWNING still lives in the house where she was born in Essex, England. The third of four children—her sister being her twin—she enjoyed the rough-and-tumble of life with two brothers as much as she did reading books. Writing came naturally as an outlet for a fertile imagination. The love of books led her to a career in libraries, and being single allowed her to take the leap into writing for a living. Success is still something of a wonder, but allows her to indulge in hobbies as varied as embroidery and bird-watching.

AMANDA BROWNING

The Bitter Price of Love

Harlequin Books

TORONTO • NEW YORK • LONDON
AMSTERDAM • PARIS • SYDNEY • HAMBURG
STOCKHOLM • ATHENS • TOKYO • MILAN
MADRID • WARSAW • BUDAPEST • AUCKLAND

ISBN 0-373-11789-2

THE BITTER PRICE OF LOVE

First North American Publication 1996.

CHAPTER ONE

IT WAS late. The party, which had been going on for hours, was slowly winding down. Finding herself temporarily alone, Reba Wyeth set down her half-empty glass and moved towards the patio door which gave access to the roof-garden of this penthouse apartment. Outside the air was cooler, free of the smoke which irritated her eyes. Down below, and as far as the eye could see, the city sparkled. New York. A faint smile curved her lips. The city was at her feet in more ways than one, so shouldn't she feel happier? She shivered and rubbed her hands up and down her bare arms. There was too much on her mind. Too much anxiety and concern. Everything was taking so long, and time was running out.

'So there you are!' a slightly scolding voice declared, and she turned, smiling at the man who came to join her.

Eliot Thorson III was universally considered to be quite a catch. He was in his late twenties, tall, tanned, with golden hair and blue eyes. Not only had he inherited a well-known chain of hotels, but he had an apartment in Manhattan and three others in LA, Paris and Rome. He also owned a string of polo ponies and an enormous yacht. Despite all of this, Reba had long ago decided he was a thoroughly nice man, whose only defect was that he was generous to a fault. She fought a constant battle to stop him showering her with anything she had shown the slightest interest in.

He also, to the dismay of her soft heart, thought he was in love with her. She didn't feel the same, and hadn't encouraged him in any way to think she might reciprocate. She could, of course, stop seeing him, but it seemed a drastic action, because he was a good friend and she enjoyed his company. She just hoped he would come to see, as she had, that it was an infatuation which would pass in time.

'It was so stuffy in there, I needed to get some fresh air,' she explained, and shivered again. It might be summer, but it could still be chilly in the small hours.

'You'll get more than fresh air; you'll catch cold,' Eliot pronounced, slipping off his dinner-jacket and placing it about her shoulders. 'There, feel better?' he asked, and when she nodded, he pulled her against him, holding her gently.

Reba didn't protest. She had never felt threatened or overwhelmed by Eliot. She liked him. Liked him a lot. 'Always the perfect gentleman,' she teased lightly.

'I'm glad you noticed,' Eliot observed wryly, then, after a long, companionable silence, added, 'When are you going to marry me, Reba?'

'Marry you?' Reba exclaimed, taken aback. This was a totally new development, and one she, rather naïvely, hadn't expected. She should have done; even though she thought it was infatuation, he didn't.

A fact he underlined now. 'Don't sound so surprised. You know I love you, don't you?'

She hated hurting people, and struggled to frame a careful reply. 'Yes, but are you sure, Eliot? You know, men fall in love with models all the time,' she said gently, hoping he would see reason.

Eliot shook his head. 'This isn't like that. I love you, Reba. I want to take care of you and make you happy. Please say you'll marry me.'

Reba eased herself free, so that she could look into his serious face. 'Oh, Eliot, I care for you very much, but I don't love you,' she pointed out unhappily.

The admission didn't dent his confidence one bit. 'You will, if you let yourself.'

She had to laugh, albeit nervously. 'You're impossible! You can't know that!'

'I know I'm in love with you, and we could be happy together,' he insisted, quartering her face with adoring eyes. 'But you're tired, aren't you, sweetheart, and not up to taking me seriously? Come on, get your purse. I'll take you home.'

Reba didn't argue, for in truth she was very nearly out on her feet, and his unexpected proposal had knocked her for six. She was glad he had let the subject drop, although she didn't believe she had heard the last of it for a moment. They said their goodbyes, and in a matter of minutes were on their way. Reba's apartment had a view over Central Park, which gave her a feeling of space in an otherwise teeming city. Eliot escorted her right to her door, opening it for her before returning her key. Yet tonight he made no move to kiss her goodnight, and his face was entirely serious.

'Listen, Reba, this is no joke. I want you to think seriously about marrying me.' His hands gripped her shoulders through his jacket as he leant forward to add weight to his words. 'I've never asked anyone else to marry me. I love you, sweetheart. We could be happy together. Think about it, please.'

She could see it was no joke. He really meant it, and the very least she could do was give it serious consideration, even if she knew she would still say no. He deserved that. 'All right, Eliot, I will think about it,' she promised.

'And you'll give me your answer when you get back from your next shoot?' he urged, not willing to let it rest having got her to this point.

She was flying off to the Caribbean tomorrow on a modelling assignment which was due to last several weeks. It would certainly give her time to think of an answer for him. 'OK. When I get back. But, Eliot, it could be no and not yes,' she warned, as she removed his jacket and held it out to him.

He took it, leaning closer. 'I'm a born optimist,' he quipped, and kissed her. 'Goodnight, sweetheart. See you in a couple of weeks.'

He left then, and Reba watched him until he disappeared into the lift with a final wave, before entering her apartment. Locking the door, she felt ... unsettled. Edgy and irritable, she made her away through to her bedroom without bothering to switch on the lights until she got there. Throwing her purse down on to the cluttered dressing-table, she removed the combs from her hair, allowing its wildness to spring free. Tossing her head, she eased the tension in her neck, and found herself studying her reflection in the glass.

It showed her what it had always shown her, but now there was added glamour. She had always been a tall, curvaceous brunette, but the right training and make-up had revealed a new Reba, whose beauty was both striking and exotic. It was her eyes which had taken her out of the common mould: large golden cat's-eyes, rimmed with long dark lashes, which gave her a felinely hungry look and added a sensual quality to her mouth.

It was the face and figure of a top model, but she hadn't considered it as a career option until, on leaving university, disaster had struck her family. Her mother had developed a crippling disease which had only one possibility of a cure—a pioneering operation in the

United States. The trouble was that it was astronomi-
cally expensive, and the family, minus a father who had
died when Reba was still quite young, couldn't afford
it.

Not, that was, until a friend, who was in the business,
had suggested that she could make a fortune as a model.
Reba hadn't even bothered to have a second thought and,
with the help of her friend, had entered the world of
modelling. In the beginning it had been an uphill
struggle, with every penny she could spare being put in
the bank to set against their expenses. Through sheer
hard work she had fought her way towards the top, never
refusing anything which would bring in money. But it
had been so slow, and it was only now, two years later,
that she was beginning to travel the world, commanding
huge sums for a single session.

It had been time they could ill afford, and it was going
to be tight getting the money for the operation before it
was too late. Unless... Suddenly she knew why she was
feeling so edgy. Eliot's proposal. It occurred to her that
if she accepted him, then it would certainly help her
family out. But that was no basis for marriage! It
wouldn't be fair. To either of them.

Eliot said he loved her, but she had never pretended
she loved him. She liked him very much, and felt they
were good friends. His kisses were pleasant and his caresses tender, but there was no spark for her. She was
twenty-three years old, and she had always thought she
would never marry anyone unless there was that certain
something between them. It wasn't ridiculous to want
the heights, only natural. She was certain that Mr Right
was out there somewhere, waiting around a corner she
had yet to turn.

But, while she was waiting for Mr Right, her mother
was slowly but surely dying—and the price of the op-

eration was going up, her conscience now reminded her. And here was Eliot, wanting to marry her. She knew they could very possibly have a happy, if unexciting, marriage. Surely she should consider it—for her mother's sake?

Sinking down on to the stool, she began cleaning off her make-up, knowing that there was no question of it. She must take it seriously though, and, however mercenary it sounded, she couldn't afford to rule out any option. Yet it wasn't going to be an easy decision to make, and she was glad she had some time in which to do it.

A week later, Reba gathered together her survival kit ready for the day's filming ahead of them, knowing she was no nearer a solution. In fact, to be honest, she knew she had been putting the moment of decision off. She had told herself she was too busy, too tired, too... Any one of a number of excuses. Now, today, glancing at her watch, she told herself it was too late to think about it.

Leaving her room in the luxury hotel which the agency had booked for them, she hurried down to the lobby where the rest of the crew would be waiting. Contrary to some people's expectations, she didn't go around dressed like a fashion-plate all the time. Today she was in cut-off shorts and a baggy Hawaiian shirt. Costume and make-up would be discussed when they reached the location.

So far she, and the other three models, had only been shot in evening-wear, but now they were moving into beach and leisurewear, and the director had decided they needed to be on a yacht for the purpose. Reba didn't mind. She loved the water and boats, although there hadn't been much time for sailing recently. Plus it would be cooler at sea. She wasn't fully acclimatised to the Caribbean heat, and sometimes found it enervating.

'Sorry I'm late,' she apologised, finding she was the last to arrive.

One of her fellow models, a Nordic blonde called Magda, who always appeared immaculately turned out, looked down her nose. 'If you get a reputation for being late, nobody is going to employ you!'

'You wish!' grinned Linda, the make-up girl, and as Magda turned away with a sniff she rolled her eyes at Reba. 'Take no notice of her, she's just jealous. You've got further quicker than she did. Plus you're going places, and she isn't. Don't let it upset you. You're going to get a lot more of the same.'

Reba smiled back gratefully. She wasn't the bitchy sort you sometimes needed to be to get on in this profession. She always tried to make friends with everyone, although Magda made that hard. 'I'll try not to, but this weather doesn't help me keep my cool. It's so hot already.'

'I heard one of the waiters saying it probably means there's going to be a storm. I'm just praying it won't come while we're at sea,' Linda groaned, then came to attention as Maurice, the director, clapped his hands loudly.

'OK, everyone, transport's here. Let's get going.'

They were ushered out to a minibus which took them from the hotel's exclusive setting to the island's main town, where the marina was situated. Reba slung her bag over her shoulder and breathed in the scent of the sea. Shading her eyes with her hands, she gazed along the lines of glittering craft of all shapes and sizes, and knew a longing to be skimming along the crystal waters, all her cares forgotten.

Maurice herded them along the main pier, then on to one of the branches. It soon became obvious that they were heading for a large white yacht where a man could be seen busily coiling rope. He glanced up as he heard them approaching, stretching to his full height, and Reba found her steps slowing, so that she was at the back of the group. She heard Maurice speaking, but it seemed to come from a great distance as she stared at the stranger.

He was tall, fair and tanned, but that wasn't what brought the sensitive hairs all over her body to attention. He was pure male power, barely leashed. His blond hair was untamed, his blue eyes wild and compelling. He took the word handsome to the edge—and beyond. His clothes were clean but well-worn, the white vest clinging to every muscled inch of his chest, down to where the low-slung denims took over, their faded cloth straining at long powerful legs and the tears at the knees only adding to his incredible presence. He exuded a potency she had never encountered before. It called to her, and she responded on a primitive level.

As if becoming aware of her gaze, his head turned, searching, and her golden eyes met and locked on to a pair of deep blue ones. All the air seemed to leave her body in a rush. She thought, I know this man. He's no stranger. I seem to have known him forever. It was the weirdest thing, and, what was more uncanny, he seemed to sense it too, for he went quite still. Without a word a message was sent and answered, and the world changed.

Maurice had been talking to the man, but he faltered when he realised he wasn't being heard, and turned to find what had caught the other man's attention. Reba was oblivious to more than one head turning, and only jolted out of the trance she appeared to be in when someone sniggered. Realising she was now the focus of everyone's attention, a hot tide of embarrassment coloured her cheeks. Her heart was thumping fit to burst, and she glanced down quickly at her feet, trying to regain her composure. What on earth had just happened?

'How sweet,' Magda drawled snidely. 'I do believe Reba has just fallen in love with the deck-hand!'

A jolt of shock ran through Reba at those words. Fallen in love? But she couldn't have! Could she? Yet what else could explain this strange excitement inside her? The fizzing of her blood which made her feel more alive than she had ever been in her life?

Was this love?

'You'd better snap out of it, Reba. Maurice looks like he's going to throw a fit,' Linda hissed in her ear, and Reba started, realising that they were the only two still left on the jetty. Everyone else was waiting on board, showing various degrees of impatience.

'Sorry,' Reba apologised, commanding her legs to move her forwards. She could feel eyes on her, but only one pair counted. A hand appeared to help her aboard, and she took it automatically, gasping as a *frisson* of electricity shot up her arm, and once more she met those incredible eyes.

'Welcome aboard,' he said easily, but there was a husky note to it, as if he had had trouble forcing the words out.

All her composure seemed to leave her in a flash. Her smile was wobbly, and her eyes questioned his, receiving an almost solar flare of emotion in return. Exhilarated and afraid all at once, she pulled free. 'Thanks,' she muttered, moving away, although it seemed incredibly hard to do.

'Hi, I'm Linda,' she heard the other girl say from behind her. 'In case you're interested, her name's Reba.'

The man's laugh was throaty and appreciative, and turned Reba's stomach into knots. 'Thanks, Linda. Hunter Jamieson.'

Hunter. She liked the sound of that. It suited him. Hunter... She daydreamed, and, for once in her life, the preparations for setting sail failed to hold her attention. In fact the whole day's shooting became something of a dream. The man called Hunter never spoke to her, nor she to him, but she was vitally aware of his presence moving around the boat. It was as if she had suddenly become attuned to his frequency, and she didn't have to look at him to know where he was.

She couldn't concentrate properly, but must have done all that was expected of her because Maurice didn't throw a tantrum. Yet it was hard to look at the camera when her eyes constantly wanted to stray. When they did, they clashed with blue ones intent on the same thing.

At the end of the day it was hard to leave the yacht, for it felt as if she were leaving part of herself behind. She had never felt this way before, and when she looked in the mirror in the privacy of her hotel room she found her cheeks were flushed and her eyes glittering. She saw a creature she no longer recognised. Every feature was the same, and yet not the same.

Of course it was impossible to sit still, and she went through the motions of preparing for dinner. She showered and washed her hair, slipping into a full-skirted, halter-necked sundress and comfortable espadrilles. However, she didn't go down to the restaurant. Her stomach was churning too much for food. Something was calling to her, something stronger than any other need. As the sun began to set, she grabbed up her purse and a thin shawl and left, obeying an instinct as old as time itself.

The harbour was still alive with people, but as she made her way through the marina she met fewer and fewer. Most were out enjoying themselves, probably having dinner, and for a moment her heart failed her as she realised Hunter might not be on the yacht. Yet she need not have worried, for as she approached the boat she saw that there was light in the cabin, and as she came alongside he appeared on deck. Without a word he held out a hand, and she put hers into it and allowed him to help her aboard.

There was a moment when they simply gazed at each other, then Hunter smiled, and used his free hand to brush away a strand of hair which the impish breeze had blown across her face.

'I knew you'd come,' he said softly, yet with a certainty she couldn't question.

'Yes,' she breathed, unable to deny it. Her eyes drank him in. Incredible to think they had only met hours ago, and yet it felt as if she had never belonged anywhere else. This evening he had changed into white chinos and a short-sleeved shirt, but they didn't disguise the powerful body beneath.

He didn't seem to mind her looking, nor did he release her hand. He studied her face as if he was imprinting it forever in his memory. 'You have amazing eyes.'

'So do you,' she returned inanely, and flushed when he laughed. Yet there was no unkindness in it, more a release from the same tension that gripped her.

'You don't act like a model.'

Reba smiled up at him. 'That's what I do, not who I am.'

A strange light flickered at the back of his eyes. 'And who are you, Reba?'

'Just a woman,' she told him simply, and watched fascinated as his mouth curved seductively as he smiled.

'Oh, I'll most definitely agree with that. You're very much a woman,' Hunter concurred huskily. 'Have you eaten?'

The prosaic question made her realise that now she was quite incredibly hungry. 'No.'

His fingers tightened on hers. 'Good. I hope you like fish.'

Belatedly she became aware that behind him a table had been set for two, and from down below came the mouth-watering aroma of cooking. 'I love it.'

Hunter dragged a hand through his hair, lips curving. 'Somehow I knew you would,' he said oddly, shaking his head before smiling again. 'Sit down, make yourself comfortable. I'll only be a moment.'

Reba caught her breath. So he felt it too, this knowing. 'Do you need any help?'

'Everything's under control. Don't run away,' he cautioned as he headed for the steps.

She wouldn't. She didn't think she could. And even if she did, something told her she would have to come back. A cliché, but true: home was where the heart was, and her heart was here. The admission didn't sound crazy or ridiculous, it just sounded right. Incredibly, amazingly right.

It was a feeling which grew all through the beautiful dinner Hunter had prepared. Someone could have dropped a bomb and it wouldn't have penetrated the cocoon which surrounded them. The outside world had ceased to exist. They talked as if it were going out of fashion. Hunter seemed to have an unquenchable need to know everything there was to know about her. She found herself telling him things she hadn't thought about for years. Afterwards, as they sipped at glasses of wine, he held her hand across the table, toying with her fingers, caressing them and twining them with his. She knew from his handling of the yacht that he was strong, yet his touch was gentle, almost as if he was afraid she would break.

Reba sighed. 'Do you realise we've talked and talked, and yet I don't even know if you have a mother?'

'I did have, but both my parents are dead now. I'm thirty-three years old, have no brothers or sisters, and I mess about with boats for a living. Your turn.'

'I'm a model, and twenty-three years old. I have a mother, but no father, and a brother and sister younger than me.'

'So your mother had to work to raise you?'

Reba nodded. 'Until she became ill. She's something of an invalid now, but she has the most amazing courage.' She hoped he wouldn't ask her more, because Harriet Wyeth was a proud woman, wanting complete control over who knew the truth of her illness. She simply refused to be pitied, and it had become second nature to her children to say nothing unless they asked her first.

Whether Hunter instinctively knew that or not, he forbore to question the statement. 'I'd like to meet her some time,' was all he said, and she squeezed his hand in relief.

'She'd like you.'

Blue eyes danced. 'Doesn't she usually like your boyfriends?'

She sent him an old-fashioned look. 'If you're asking me if I have one, the answer is no.' She had a fleeting thought for Eliot, but dismissed it.

'Good,' he pronounced gruffly, and her heart flipped over. Almost in the same instant she yawned, and Hunter looked at his watch. 'Do you realise it's gone one o'clock? I'd better get you back to the hotel. You need your beauty sleep,' he declared, releasing her hand only to come round and help her to her feet, handing her her purse and draping her shawl about her shoulders.

'Funny, but I don't feel in the least bit tired,' Reba pronounced, and immediately yawned again.

Hunter helped her down to the jetty with a laugh. 'Something tells me Maurice won't be pleased if you end up with bags under your eyes. I don't want him deciding to use another boat. Then I'll hardly get to see you.' He slipped his arm round her shoulders and urged her towards the shore.

Reba decided she had never felt so secure. 'Do you want to see me again?' she asked, half teasing, half serious.

'Only all the time,' Hunter admitted wryly, and prompted a confession which had been bubbling inside her all day.

'You'll think it's crazy, but I feel as if I've known you all my life.'

Hunter came to a halt, raising her chin with his hand so that their eyes met. 'It's not crazy, Reba. I feel the same. The minute I saw you, I knew you were different,' he said, and brought his mouth down to cover hers.

It was a gentle kiss, offering much in its infinite tenderness. It was a promise of things to come, a seal on words unspoken. It took her heart away, and returned it to her irrevocably altered.

He released her with a shaken sigh. 'This is uncanny. This morning I was a normal, level-headed man. Now I don't seem to know which way is up any more.'

Oh, she knew just how he felt. Nothing had prepared her for this. Nothing ever could. 'Do you mind?'

'Hell, no! I've waited all my life for you; I'm not going to run away now.'

Her heart seemed to swell in her chest. It didn't matter that they had only just met. Something that was destined to be could take five minutes or fifty years, but it *would* happen. She knew in her soul that they had been meant to meet.

Hunter left her at the hotel entrance, driving her there in a beat-up Jeep which had been parked behind one of the waterfront bars. Not wanting the evening to be over, Reba turned to him just as he was reaching for her, and this time the kiss was different. It sought a response to a passion held in check. Tasting her, learning her, he took her breath away and sent her blood pulsing through her veins. That unspoken awareness which had been between them all evening came to the surface at last, and she gasped, feeling nerve-ends come alive which she hadn't even known existed. There was no way of not returning the kiss, and no way of hiding her groan of dismay when it ended all too soon.

Hunter's breathing was ragged too, as he ran a finger over her tingling lips. 'Momma should have told me it could be like this,' he said huskily on a broken laugh, breaking the nerve-twisting tension, and Reba sighed, relaxing.

'Do you realise you haven't asked me about my girlfriends?'

Somehow the thought didn't worry her. 'How many have you had?'

His chuckle did wonderful things to her pulse-rate. 'Plenty—in the past. Now there's only you, and I want you all to myself. Do you mind?' Hunter sounded possessive, and it sent a thrill along her spine.

'No.' She didn't want to share him either. She wanted to be alone with him, close to him. A minute without him would seem a minute wasted.

'Don't leave with the others tomorrow. Stay aboard, and we'll sail up the coast. What do you say?'

She smiled. 'Yes.'

Hunter groaned. 'The way you say that! It's going to be a hell of a long day.'

Laughing, she climbed down from the vehicle. It *would* be a long day, but eventually it would be over, and then there would be just the two of them. She liked the sound of that. Liked it very much indeed.

They were both right; it did seem to take forever, but finally, after a successful day's filming, the crew and the models were packed up and ready to leave. Reba had wished them gone a thousand times, because she hadn't been able to speak to Hunter above twice all day. Every hour the need had grown inside her to be near to him, to touch him. She'd never really understood why couples felt they had to be glued together, but now she knew. It was a compulsive need to make contact, even if that simply meant holding hands.

'They're gone,' Hunter declared from behind her, and she spun round, not having heard him come down to the cabin which they had been using as a changing-room.

A lump constricted her throat as she finally came face to face with him. There was a glitter in his eyes, and a teasing curve to his lips which made her heart flip. 'I thought they'd never go!' she exclaimed, wanting to go to him, yet strangely held back. She didn't realise how vulnerable she looked in jeans and T-shirt, with her face free of make-up.

'Come and kiss me, Reba, before I go quietly insane,' he ordered huskily, and she knew then that he had suffered as much as she had.

She positively flew across the room and into his arms. All day she had been longing for his kiss and, from the hunger in his own lips which fused with hers, she knew she hadn't been alone. Lord, she hadn't imagined it, this tingling pleasure that sent pulses to every corner of her body, bringing it alive as never before. He was holding her so tightly that she could scarcely breathe, but it was wonderful.

Hunter reluctantly lifted his head before they suffocated. 'I needed that,' he groaned feelingly, and his fingers curled into her hair, bringing her head down on to his shoulder.

She could hear his heart thudding wildly, and revelled in it. 'I missed you.'

He laughed. 'God, this is crazy. We're behaving like a couple of teenagers!'

Reba laughed with him, a bubbling sound, feeling almost drunk with happiness. 'You know something? I don't care.'

'Neither do I. Come on, let's get under way.'

They worked together as if they had always been a team. Reba didn't need to be told what to do, jumping to each task with pleasure. It was hard work, but she enjoyed every aspect of sailing, even the most mundane job. When the sails were set and they were skimming along, leaving a creamy wake behind them, she joined Hunter at the wheel, slipping her arm through his.

He bent and pressed a kiss to her wind-blown hair. 'You look at home here.'

It felt like the greatest compliment, coming from a man who seemed at one with the craft and the sea. 'I love sailing, but I've never sailed a yacht as lovely as this. She handles beautifully—it makes me itch to have a go.'

He grinned, stepping back. 'Then she's all yours.'

With a cry of alarm, Reba sprang for the wheel, bringing the yacht's nose into the wind again, watching the sail billow out. 'That was a nasty trick!'

'I wouldn't have done it if I didn't trust you,' Hunter returned, laughing. 'Keep her on that course and try not to hit anything!'

She poked her tongue out at him, then laughed, buoyed up by his compliment. The wind tugged at her hair, and the spray caught her face, but she was on cloud nine. As far as she was concerned, they could sail on forever and never stop, so long as they were together.

However, they put in at a small uninhabited bay not too far along the coast and dropped anchor. Dinner was simple—chicken, French bread, cheese, fruit and white wine—but food had never tasted better. Afterwards they stretched out along the seat-cushion, finishing off the wine.

'Where did you learn to sail?' Hunter asked, settling her more comfortably into the curve of his arm.

'My father was a sailor. He encouraged me, and later on I joined our local sailing club,' she explained, trying not to be so vitally aware of his strong body pressed along the length of hers. But it was impossible. Little fires flickered into life all through her, and she wanted nothing more than to turn and press herself closer, to explore the flats and planes his clothes only hinted at.

'Why did you take up modelling?' Ever so gently his free hand began caressing a line up and down her arm.

Reba recalled the reason with a twist of her heart. She wanted to explain, but her mother preferred to keep her illness a secret within the family. Although she knew Hunter was trustworthy, she still couldn't break her promise. 'I didn't intend to, but a friend told me I could make a lot of money at it, so I changed my mind.' It was the truth, as far as it went.

Hunter's hand left her arm to go to her chin and raise it so that he could see her face. He was frowning. 'Is it so important to make a lot of money?'

She shrugged, trying to make light of it. 'Of course, if you don't have any. Only the rich can say money isn't important, and that's because they have more than enough for their needs.' Her eyes clouded over. 'Sometimes our needs are bigger than our pockets.'

'Mmm, you may be right,' he conceded, then, in an abrupt change of mood, set his glass down and relieved her of her own. Getting to his feet, he held out his hand. 'Dance with me.'

Bemused, she automatically allowed him to pull her up and into his arms. 'There isn't any music,' she protested as he slowly began to move.

'Sure there is. Just close your eyes and listen,' Hunter argued, pulling her closer until there was no air between them. They fitted as if they had been made two halves of a whole, and as her head came to rest on his shoulder, eyes closing, she began to hear the music.

Her free hand travelled up to his nape, fingers curling into the thickness of his hair. She could feel his lips on her own hair, slowly fanning downwards to her eye and her cheek, and it was simplicity itself to raise her head the fraction needed for their lips to meet. She heard music of a different kind then, at the first gentle caress. He sipped at her, tasting her sweetness, and her lips softened, moving to his command, parting at the silken glide of his tongue.

Everything vanished. There was only this exquisite sensation, the gentle exploration slowly building up a powerful need to act and not just react. Her tongue moved, touching his, and the sensation was electric. She gasped, pressing closer, boldly seeking more and more as his kiss became increasingly demanding. They fed off each other, and what had started so gently soon became a conflagration.

Reba had never experienced anything like it. Nobody had ever made her feel like this, arousing a need that throbbed inside her. As his hands found their way beneath her T-shirt her legs very nearly gave out. His touch was scorching her. She was going up in flames! And yet she wanted to burn. She wanted to feel his hands on her body, and she wanted to explore him the same way. The first brush of his thumbs along the swell of her breasts brought a whimper of the purest pleasure to her lips, and when he finally cupped her bounty, stroking her nipples into aching buds, she shuddered and her head fell back helplessly as she arched towards him.

'Hunter!' His name was an ache of need. She had no doubts, no fears. She gladly gave herself over to him, trusting him implicitly not to hurt her. Anything he wanted, she wanted. He was the lover she had dreamt of. He would take her to the heights and keep her safe. She loved him.

'No!' Hunter drew his hands away, and her drugged brain registered that they were trembling as he smoothed her T-shirt back down. Gazing into her bewildered eyes, he smiled crookedly. 'No, Reba. This is too fast. God knows, I want you, but I want to get to know you first. I want us to go slowly, savour everything, not rush on as if there were no tomorrow. When we finally make love it will be all the better for waiting, I promise.'

Reba felt choked. She had been importuned all her adult life by men who wanted only one thing from her, and now here was the one man she would gladly have given herself to, with no regrets, saying they should wait. It made her feel cherished, and she knew he really cared for her.

Her eyes glittered brightly with tears that knew nothing of pain. 'All right,' she agreed, and sighed as his arms closed around her. 'After all, we've got all the time in the world.'

CHAPTER TWO

THE ten days which followed became a period of time Reba would never forget. Even in her darkest moments, they would hold a warmth and brilliance that could never be dimmed. It was a time of discovery, as much about herself as about Hunter. She discovered what it was like to be truly happy. The fact that that happiness was totally bound up with another person didn't worry her, because she knew that what was true for her was true for him also.

Outside work, they became virtually inseparable. At first she was teased unmercifully, but when it became apparent that there was more here than just a passing flirtation, the company grew silent, watching the romance unfolding before them with equal measures of warmth and envy.

Apart from a shared love of sailing, which they indulged almost every day, sailing a short way round the island at evening to have dinner in their own private cove, they also discovered an equal love and concern for nature. They held long discussions on the way natural habitats were being destroyed, and what they could do to put the world right. Other times they took long walks along the silver beaches, or went inland, where Hunter introduced her to the joys of bird-watching.

They spent every available hour together, exploring the island and enjoying each other's company. To an outsider it might have looked platonic, but they were fully aware that underlying everything was that banked-down passion. Reba found it added spice to everything they did. It was something special to wait for, to savour, and their goodnight kisses were a pleasurable torture. She knew, beyond any doubt, that she loved him, and was as certain as she could be that he loved her. He didn't have to say it. He had a way of being able to tell her with the briefest of touches, or just a look or smile. He made her heart sing.

Yet the banked fires in his eyes made her shiver in anticipation. His control was awesome, all the more so when, as the days passed, hers became less and less in evidence. Her dreams became extremely erotic as she fantasised about what would happen when that control finally snapped.

She found out in a rush when the shoot on the yacht ended. Their next location was to be up in the hills somewhere, near a waterfall. A week there, and then the assignment was over. For the first time Reba became uncertain. Hunter had to know the assignment wouldn't last forever, and yet he had said nothing. She had made tentative arrangements to remain behind, though not at the hotel. She had hoped she could persuade Hunter to allow her to stay on the yacht, but his silence made her hesitate to ask.

Perhaps she would broach the subject tonight, she thought, as she showered and changed into a brilliantly hued sarong she had picked up in the market. As had become habit, she had stayed on board when the others left, and was just gathering everything up into her bag when the door behind her crashed open. She spun round in alarm, finding Hunter advancing on her with a thunderous face.

'So!' He snatched the bag from her hands and emptied it out again on the bunk. 'You are leaving! Just when were you going to tell me, Reba?' he demanded, in a voice which threatened to topple small mountains.

Her mouth dropped open in sheer surprise. 'What?'

She could have sworn that she heard his teeth grind. 'Don't give me that. I've just spent the last ten minutes being thanked for my services and told goodbye!'

She understood then, and bit her lip to stop herself smiling. 'Hunter, will you please calm down,' she ordered, feeling a bubble of laughter rise up inside her. Oh Lord, he'd never forgive her if she laughed.

'Give me one good reason why I should?' he demanded loudly.

'Because I'm not leaving!' she shouted back equally loudly, and watched him falter to a halt.

'You're not leaving?' He asked for confirmation much more quietly.

Reba had to bring her hand up to cover her twitching lips. 'We're going to another location, not leaving the island. At least, not yet,' she explained, and watched in fascination as a tide of colour rose up his neck. Then, of course, she did laugh. She simply couldn't help it.

Something primeval burst into life at the back of his eyes, and he advanced on her. 'So you think it's funny, do you? Let's see how you like this!' With a squeal she tried to avoid him, but he was too quick for her. Tossing her over his shoulder, he carried her struggling body along to the master cabin. Shutting the door with his foot, he tossed her down on the bed and came down after her, pinning her to the covers with the weight of his body.

In a flash everything changed. Reba's eyes grew huge as she stared up at him, seeing the softening of his face, the sensuous curve of his lips. 'Is this the punishment?' she whispered thickly, feeling her blood begin to pump heavily through her veins.

Hunter's eyes dropped to her lips, and they parted in anticipation of his kiss. 'Hell, no. This is the prize.

Somewhere along the line I must have done something good, and you're my reward. I'm never going to let you go.'

With that he lowered his mouth to hers and, as she welcomed him, she knew that this time there was to be no turning back. Passion rose swiftly. She couldn't recall who undressed whom. Perhaps they undressed each other. All she knew was that at last they were free of all restrictions, because flesh burned flesh as they moved together. Love taught her what to do as she travelled this new path. It gave her pleasure to run her hands over the sweat-slicked planes of his shoulders and back, feeling the heat of him, glorying in the way he moaned and arched into her. It was wondrous to find that he experienced the same pleasures at her touch as she did at his caresses, and her hands flitted upwards, finding the flat male nipples and teasing them until she heard him catch his breath.

He fell back against the pillow, his magnificent body open to her hot gaze. She didn't see the way his eyes glittered through the slits of his lashes as she embarked on a voyage of discovery. Where her hand roamed, her lips followed, tasting him, knowing him. She heard him sigh and move, felt his hand come down to tangle in her hair, but when she would have made her final conquest his fingers tightened and pulled her upwards until he rolled over, pinioning her again.

'God, you're a witch. You take me to the limits of my control.'

'I want you to lose it,' Reba gasped, as his mouth trailed a fiery path down her throat.

'Not yet, tiger-eyes, not yet,' he growled, and set about making her lose hers instead.

It didn't take long, with his hands and lips exploring every inch of her. Soon she was writhing against him as his mouth teased her breasts. His tongue laved her nipples even as his teeth nipped, and as her hands rose to hold him to her he drew her aching flesh into the warm cavern of his mouth and suckled until she cried out her pleasure.

He taught her body to sing, playing it like a finely tuned instrument, bringing her from one peak to the next, yet always leaving her aching for the summit which seemed beyond her reach. But then, magically, it wasn't. His seeking hands found the warm, moist centre of her, stroking her until she arched and froze as a myriad stars exploded behind her closed eyes. And as she floated somewhere beyond herself he moved over her, parting her thighs with his, entering her slowly, breaking the last tie to her former self. He transported her upwards on a coil of tension which grew and grew with every thrust of the powerful body which had finally lost control, until there was nowhere else to go and the world exploded in unimaginable pleasure.

The universe righted itself very slowly as Reba raised eyelids which seemed to be weighted. She was curled into the warmth of Hunter's side, and with a sigh she realised that they were lying on the bed in the master cabin of the yacht, in the aftermath of the most exquisite loving. She couldn't remember ever being so happy. Her head rested on Hunter's chest while his fingers idly combed their way through her damp hair. She loved the sound of his heart beating; it was so solid and reassuring.

'How do you feel?' There was concern in his voice. Even in his passion, he had recognised that it was her first time.

'Wonderful,' she breathed, knowing she might ache tomorrow, but not caring.

'I didn't hurt you?'

She lifted her head then, lips twisting in a wry grin. 'I can't remember.'

Hunter grinned back. 'I was that good, hmm?'

She dug her chin into his shoulder, making him wince. 'Don't get big-headed. I have nothing to compare it with, remember?'

He tweaked her nose. 'Never mind, I have. On a scale of one to ten, I'd say you were——' He broke off as her fingers threatened a tender spot, laughing as he rolled her over. 'Jealous?'

Her confidence was high. 'Should I be?'

'No,' Hunter confessed at once, propping himself on one elbow and smoothing her damp hair away from her face. 'We've got to make some plans, tiger-eyes,' he declared softly, and her heart galloped on apace as she anticipated what plans he meant. A tiny smile hugged the curve of her lips as her finger found the dimple in his chin.

'What plans are those?'

He caught her hand, kissing the tip of each finger in turn. 'You said you'd have to leave eventually.'

'I can stay a little longer, if you'll let me stay on the yacht.' She put forward her plans hopefully.

'But you'll still have to leave, right?' he added, his face losing some of its softness.

Reba licked her lips. 'I have to work, Hunter. What else can I do?'

Blue eyes bored into hers. 'You could marry me,' he suggested, and they were the most wonderful words she had ever heard, bar three yet unspoken.

'Oh, Hunter, I'd love to marry you. Whenever you say!' she cried, flinging herself against him as tears moistened her eyes. Yet even in the midst of her happiness, reality intruded. 'But I'll still have to work.'

He smiled into her wet eyes. 'No, you won't. Let me do the worrying about money. I might mess about with boats for a living, but it is a living. I can support my own wife.'

Of course he could, but he didn't understand the situation. She knew he would when she explained to him, and she would do that as soon as she had her mother's permission. It was important to Harriet Wyeth to feel she was in control of some of her life, and although Reba knew she could tell him now, she felt she couldn't betray a trust. Besides, it would only be for one day. As long as it took to make a phone call. Then they would work something out. Two people who loved each other as much as they did would always be able to work out their problems together.

'All right, Hunter, whatever you say.'

Hunter groaned, his smile rueful. 'Lord, if only I could be as certain you'd always be this docile, tiger-eyes.'

'Never mind. It doesn't matter how uppity I might get, you'll always be able to make me purr,' she tantalised, and pulled his head down to hers.

Not surprisingly, it was late when Hunter dropped Reba off at her hotel. He had wanted her to stay over but, with the shoot moving on, she knew she would have to be up early. So they parted reluctantly at the entrance, where she kissed him goodnight and hurried inside. When she went to collect her key from the night clerk, he handed it to her, together with a folded piece of paper.

'There is a message for you, Miss Wyeth. Somebody tried to contact you earlier, but we did not know where you were.'

Icy fingers of dread trailed themselves up Reba's spine. So far as she knew there was only one reason anyone would want to contact her urgently. Sure enough, the message was from her sister, asking her to ring home at once.

'Thank you,' she managed to say, before hurrying to the lift.

Once in her room, she threw down her bag and picked up the telephone. The wonders of modern science meant it wasn't long before she heard the sound of ringing, and then came her sister's voice.

'Maggie? It's Reba,' she began, and was interrupted at once.

'Where have you been?' her sister demanded in a distraught voice. 'It's been hours and hours!'

Reba closed her eyes and drew in a shaky breath. Revealing her exact whereabouts was out of the question, even to her sister. 'I've only just got your message. Calm down, Maggie, and tell me what's wrong,' she ordered, trying to remain calm herself.

Down the line came the sound of several sniffs. 'Mum took a turn for the worse. Oh, Reba, they had to take her in again! The doctor said I should contact you, just in case...'

Just in case! Reba's fingers tightened on the telephone wire. 'All right, I understand. Is she stable?'

'Yes, but she was unconscious for such a long time. I was frightened, Reba,' Maggie exclaimed, on the verge of tears again.

'Of course you were, darling. Now, listen to me, Maggie, I'll be coming home just as soon as I can. First I have some...arrangements to make. I'll let you know what flight I'll be on just as soon as I know myself. If Mum's stable, then nothing is going to happen just yet, so do try to stop worrying. I'll be there, I promise.'

She did her very best to reassure her younger sister before she rang off, but the truth of the matter was that she desperately needed reassurance herself. Suddenly, from walking on a cloud, she plunged into the pit of despair. Every time her mother suffered another setback, the chances of the operation being in time lessened. Which meant it had to take place now. They couldn't afford to wait any longer.

She dropped her head in her hands. Oh, God, why now? Why now, when she had just met the most wonderful man, who loved her as much as she loved him, and wanted to marry her? Her heart cried out to marry him, and it was that very same heart which broke as she was forced to admit she couldn't afford to. Hunter might be a wonderful man, but he couldn't possibly help her mother when her need was so great! They needed money, and the only way she knew of to get it was to accept Eliot's proposal. Eliot, whom she hadn't thought of for weeks, was suddenly the answer to her prayers. She knew he was not the kind of man to refuse to help her. He would probably offer to pay without asking for any security, because he loved her. Yet it was precisely because he loved her that she couldn't ask without making a commitment. She could only accept his help by accepting his proposal.

The knowledge brought with it a shattering pain. Why must she be tortured this way? Torn between love and duty. It wasn't fair! But if she refused to help her mother now, she knew she would never forgive herself, because to do so would be passing the death sentence on her. She groaned in despair. Yet to marry Eliot when she was in love with another man... How could she do that? How could she possibly give Hunter up?

Back and forth the arguments battled inside her mind all night, wearing away at her spirit. By dawn she knew it was hopeless. She knew she would have to destroy something wonderful whatever course she chose. By the time the sun was above the horizon, she accepted she had no choice. She never had had. She loved both her mother and Hunter, but one had to be sacrificed. There wasn't even a contest. Her mother would die, but Hunter wouldn't. He would live on and get over her, if somehow she could make him hate her enough. There had to be a way, something bad enough to turn love to hate, because she couldn't tell him that, although she loved him, would love him till she died, she was going to marry someone else.

If only he had been rich, like Eliot! But it was no use thinking like that. If-onlys were for fools. Hunter wasn't rich, he was simply who he was, and she couldn't tear his pride to shreds too by telling him he simply wasn't rich enough to help her. She had to leave him something. Pride would get him through, as it must get her through the ordeal ahead.

The painful decision made, she felt curiously numb as she showered and changed into the cream linen trouser-suit she used for travelling. Then it was only a matter of waiting until a reasonable hour before picking up the telephone again. First she made arrangements for a flight to be booked for her, then asked to be put through to Maurice's room.

'Hello?' the director barked, patently annoyed at being roused so early.

'This is Reba, Maurice. Sorry, but I've had an urgent call from home. There's been an emergency. I'm going to have to leave.' She waited for the explosion she expected, and wasn't disappointed.

'You're what? No way, toots. Absolutely no way are you walking out on this!'

His anger didn't alarm her; she felt too numb. Her eyes travelled to the window, and it didn't surprise her to see that the sun had disappeared. The sea looked angry and the wind had risen dramatically. Her lips twisted. Somehow it suited her mood. 'I'll be leaving on the first available flight,' she told him bluntly.

'You do that, toots, and I'm gonna make sure you never work in this burg again!' Maurice threatened, slamming the phone down.

So much for that, she thought wearily as she replaced the receiver. She doubted if he had the clout to carry out his threat, but then she didn't think she would be working for long anyway. Sighing, she crossed to the dressing-table. She had done the easy bit, now came the hard part. To do it she would need to look her best. She couldn't let one iota of her inner misery show when she went to see Hunter. Fortunately she had been taught to use make-up to its full advantage, and the result was near-perfect. Now, if she could only manage a smile, she might just be able to pull off the acting job of her life!

Even when the taxi dropped her off at the marina, she still didn't know what she would say. Her mind seemed to have gone blank. Not so her heart. It thrummed out a sickening beat as she traversed the jetties towards her goal. Hunter was there, working on deck, and he looked up when he heard footsteps, surprise then pleasure crossing his face by turns.

Jumping ashore, he waited for her to join him. 'Hey, this is a nice surprise. I thought you'd be miles away by now.'

Training came to her aid, giving her the ability to smile through her pain. 'I should have been, but there was a technical hitch. I have the morning off.' The first lie, but who the hell was counting?

Hunter reached out a long arm, hooking her waist and pulling her into his arms. 'Their loss is my gain, tiger-eyes,' he growled and brought his head down to hers.

Reba kissed him with a desperate passion, knowing this was probably the very last time she would ever share something so wonderful. Tears scalded the backs of her eyes, but she beat them back. Then, unable to take any more, she dragged her mouth free, burying her head against his shoulder while her mind sought desperately for a way out.

'What are you doing to the boat?' she asked, noticing piles of gear stacked on deck, and using it as an excuse to ease away from him.

Hunter still managed to keep an arm around her, but he turned towards the yacht. 'Jim Mitchell, the owner, has finally decided he'll pick her up in Trinidad, so I'm getting her ready to sail down.'

Reba caught her breath, as sudden inspiration came to her. It wouldn't be nice, but it was what she was looking for. She had known the agency had arranged the use of a millionaire's yacht for the shoot, and that Hunter certainly wasn't him. But what if she pretended she *had* thought that? What if she pretended she was that worst kind of woman—a gold-digger? Surely then he would turn against her, and, in the end, forget her?

She didn't have to pretend shock; just the thought of what she was about to do had driven all colour from her face. She knew this was going to hurt her more than it would him, and it seemed to take an awful effort to find her voice. 'Jim Mitchell's yacht?' she queried faintly.

At first Hunter didn't register the strain in her voice. 'He owns the company who owns the fashion-house you're advertising. That's how you got to use the yacht for your shoot.'

Deep inside her her soul screamed, as if it had just been dragged down into hell. He was making it so easy for her. Stiffly, as if she had suddenly aged a hundred years, Reba made herself face him. Lord, I'm so cold. So cold. 'But... I thought this was your yacht?' she said sharply, embarking on what she knew was going to be a living nightmare.

Her tone reached him now, and he frowned. His eyes scanned her, noting her paleness. There was a strange silence before he spoke. 'Did you?' he asked, and she had never heard that quality in his voice before.

The very flatness in the tone of those two words spoke volumes. He was way ahead of her now. She sensed it. A pain so fierce that it twisted her up almost brought a moan to her lips. Oh God, Hunter, I love you. Forgive me. Hands bunched into fists, she made herself sound angry, as if she were the aggrieved party. 'You certainly acted as if you owned it!'

Hunter went still. His blue eyes had become shuttered, and when he spoke his voice cut like cold steel. 'I see. You thought I was a rich man, didn't you?' A violent anger entered his eyes as he shook his head. 'Boy, did you have me fooled. I actually thought you loved me too.'

Love him? She loved him so much she thought she might die from the pain. But she couldn't. She had to shrug and wave her hand dismissively. 'Of course I *loved* you, but...' She let the word hang tellingly.

His beautiful mouth turned ugly. 'But only because I was a rich man? Tell me, precisely what did you think messing about with boats meant?'

She had to swallow hard in order to answer. 'That you owned the thing, of course!'

'And so you thought you had it made when I asked you to marry me.'

She was going to shatter. Every hope and dream she had ever had was here, coalesced into this one man— and she couldn't have him. It took every ounce of her courage to add to the lie. 'I told you how important money was. I made up my mind a long time ago to marry a rich man.'

The love which had once blazed from his eyes was gone forever, replaced by a searing contempt. 'Whether you love him or not?'

Every look and word was a blade to cut her with. She was amazed that he couldn't see she was dying inside. She felt as if her emotions were written in neon. Yet her shrug was a perfect gem of indifference. 'Naturally I'd prefer to love him. When I met you——'

'You thought you'd hit the jackpot!' Hunter interrupted harshly, then abruptly moved away from her, as if the closeness would taint him. 'Sorry, sweetheart, but you just lucked out.'

Reba clung to her small victory as if it were a lifeline. Her words had worked. Already he hated her. Despair like she had never known threatened to overtake her, but she couldn't give in to it. Now, or ever. 'You win some, you lose some.'

Her words drew a glance so cold she flinched. 'That's your philosophy, is it?'

If only it were! Unfortunately she didn't have another flip answer in her right then. 'What are you going to do?' she asked finally.

'Does it matter? I'll probably put out, but wherever I go, it certainly won't be where the rich hang out. I intend to go and get royally drunk, and thank my lucky stars I'm not rich, because I've just had a lucky escape from the greediest little gold-digger it's ever been my misfortune to meet!' he growled at her.

She caught back a sob by pressing her hand to her lips. 'I do love you in my way, Hunter,' she managed to say, wanting to tell him, even if he no longer listened.

His lip curled. 'Sweetheart, you don't know what love is. If you did, you wouldn't have just thrown it all away. I don't know who I pity most—you, or the man you eventually manage to snare. One day you're going to find out money isn't everything, Reba,' he told her, and without another word he swung himself back on board and disappeared below.

Knowing her composure was about to desert her, Reba retraced her steps on legs which threatened to give out at any minute. She had done what she had set out to do, but there was no joy in the knowledge. Her whole body ached with the pain of her betrayal, but she hoped that one day he would thank her for what she had done. At least she had the satisfaction of knowing he wouldn't go on wanting someone he could never have.

Hailing a cruising taxi, she collapsed inside and asked to be taken back to the hotel. She glanced at her watch, amazed to see that barely an hour had passed. Hysteria brought a lump to lodge in her throat. It had taken less than an hour to bring her world down around her. Somehow she had to salvage what she could and go on, but she knew she would never see Hunter again, and her heart was a dead thing inside her.

Then began her dark night of the soul. Back in her hotel room, she flung herself down on the bed and cried until there were no more tears left. In the state of numbness which followed, she told herself that there had been nothing else she could do. Too much rested on her, and she couldn't selfishly abandon her mother to her fate. She loved Hunter. He was the best thing that had ever happened to her. She had done the only thing she could for him, by making him hate her.

But it didn't ease the pain. It would take months, even years, to make thinking about him halfway bearable.

Emotionally drained, she knew she would have to put on the second greatest act of her life in the next few days. Eliot at least didn't expect a wild display of affection from her, but she would have to show him she was happy in her choice. She hadn't decided when she would ask him for his help. That would depend on how she found her mother.

Harriet was the one who had to believe that Reba was happy. Neither she, nor the rest of the family, must ever know the sacrifice she had made. She knew her mother would blame herself for ruining her daughter's life, and that was a situation Reba was determined to avoid. So, to all appearances, this marriage would be for love and no other reason.

At least that gave her a purpose, a reason to go on, and she flew home to England later that day, determined to appear happy. The house was empty when she reached it the following day, but Maggie had left her a note saying she had gone to the hospital, and that there was salad in the fridge for her if she wanted it. Having forced herself to eat on the plane, she only lingered long enough to wash and redo her make-up before driving herself to the hospital in the car she had left garaged at the house.

She called in to see the doctor first, and he was characteristically cautious.

'As you know, every one of these attacks worsens her condition. Your mother is a very resilient woman, and she fights back every time, but it cannot go on indefinitely. The operation will still be able to help her so long as it takes place fairly soon. However, there will come a time when it is no longer viable, especially should she be unable to travel.'

This was pretty much what Reba had expected to hear, and it helped her to know that her decision had been the right one. 'I expect to get the money very soon. If the operation was to take place within the next two or three months, that would still be OK, wouldn't it?' she queried, needing to know precisely. Either she asked Eliot before they were married, or after. Lord, just how did she go about asking for so large an amount?

The doctor pursed his lips. 'I should think the sooner the better. Our best hope is that your mother doesn't have another attack too soon.'

That was it then. It must be before the wedding. 'I'll have the money next week. Please go ahead and make all the arrangements.'

The doctor looked taken aback, but he rallied at once, not looking a gift horse in the mouth. 'That's good news. I'll put the wheels in motion then, and let you know when everything is ready.'

'Thank you, Doctor.' Reba's own smile was tight, but he didn't seem to notice. She went off in search of her mother then, finding her in a small ward that took four beds, two of which were empty at present.

'Reba!' Maggie was out of her seat as soon as she saw her sister's head appear round the door. She was shorter than Reba, her hair browner and her eyes more hazel, but she was just as beautiful, in a less exotic way. 'Thank goodness you've arrived.'

They hugged each other warmly, then Reba glanced over at the bed. 'How is she?'

'Better. The doctor says she may go home soon. I told her you were coming. She ticked me off!'

Reba smiled. 'Then she must be better.'

Maggie grinned, as much in relief as amusement. 'I'll go and get you some coffee, shall I? I expect you'll want to talk to her on your own for a bit.'

'Actually I want to talk to you both, so don't be long,' she disagreed, and moved to her mother's bedside as Maggie left the room.

Harriet Wyeth looked pale and drawn as she lay against her pillows, but her eyes were as sharp as ever as she looked up at her eldest child.

'I told Maggie she shouldn't have sent for you,' she protested.

Reba bent down to kiss her mother's cheek, then sat down in the chair her sister had vacated. 'I'm glad she did. I would have come anyway. I've some news for you.'

Harriet pulled herself a little higher up the pillow. 'Good news?'

'The very best,' she agreed, taking her mother's hand and squeezing it gently.

'What have I missed?' Maggie demanded to know, returning just then with the coffee which she set down on the locker.

'Nothing, darling,' Harriet assured her at once. 'Reba was just saying she's got some good news for us. Tell us, dear, or Maggie is going to burst.'

'I will not!' Maggie protested, but she looked across avidly at her sister all the same.

Reba licked her lips. She had prepared what she was going to say during the endless flight, and now hoped she could pull it off. 'Well, I didn't like to say anything before I went away, but this assignment brought us very near the total we need. Then I managed to earn some bonuses too, so the good news is that you should be having your operation very soon, Mum!' she announced, and the look on her mother's face was reward enough for all her own sorrow.

'Oh, Reba!' Her mother's soft exclamation was drowned out by Maggie's squeal of delight, quickly followed by a sudden rush of tears.

'Are you pleased?'

Harriet's fingers tightened on her daughter's. 'Of course I am, but for your sake. You've worked so hard, and I never thought it was fair to ask so much of you. I've longed to be able to get up and help. I've felt so angry and helpless! But now you can stop and get on with your own life.'

'Mum, if you could get up and walk, you would. We all know that,' Maggie said as she wiped her eyes.

'And I am going to get on with my life,' Reba added quickly. 'That's my other piece of news. I'm going to get married.' There, it was out, and she hadn't made a mess of it—yet.

Harriet Wyeth's surprise quickly changed to delight. 'Married? Why, Reba, that's wonderful news. Who is it? Do I know him?'

'His name is Eliot, Mother. Eliot Thorson the Third, to be exact. You don't know him, but I'm hoping you'll meet him soon.'

Her mother's eyes widened. 'Good heavens, with a name like that, he sounds well off.'

Reba laughed, even as she felt heat invade her cheeks. 'Actually, his family does happen to own one of the largest hotel chains in the States,' she enlightened them calmly, hoping they would mistake guilt for self-consciousness.

'Do you love him very much, Reba?' Harriet asked softly.

Love him? In an instant Reba's mind threw up the picture of a pair of intense blue eyes, before the need for self-preservation made her blank it out. They weren't for her, and right now she couldn't allow herself to remember that pain.

'Yes, I love him. Eliot's a wonderful man.' The lie tripped easily off her tongue. She was getting good at it. 'You'll like him.'

Harriet smiled. 'Of course I will. I'll like any man who loves you and can make you happy, Reba. It's been my dearest wish that you should fall in love one day,' she added gently, unwittingly opening a wound that could never heal.

Pain caught Reba unprepared, and she was glad her watery eyes and smile were misinterpreted. 'Everything is turning out right after all, isn't it?' she said gruffly. 'We're fighters and survivors, and we've won through.'

Harriet Wyeth laughed through her own tears. 'Yes, darling, we have. And now you're going to do something for yourself and be happy, Reba.'

Reba uttered a choked laugh. 'I will be. Marrying Eliot will make me happy. Very, very happy,' she insisted firmly.

'So when is the wedding to be, and can I be bridesmaid?' Maggie asked, grinning all over her face because her world had been miraculously brightened.

Reba pulled a wry face. 'We haven't decided. Actually, Eliot doesn't even know I've accepted.' Seeing their two startled expressions, she eased in yet another lie. 'You see, he asked me before this assignment, and although I would have said yes, Eliot insisted I take this time to make sure. I had to see you first—that's why I've told you. I'm going to fly back to New York and tell him myself, now that I know you're OK.' This was make or break. If her mother should smell a rat...

But she didn't; she merely shook her head and laughed. 'You young people do things in the most crazy way! Now, take a deep breath and tell me all about him.'

With her boats well and truly burned, Reba could do nothing else but accept the invitation with all the enthusiasm she could muster. Perhaps if she told herself she would be happy often enough, one day it might even come true.

CHAPTER THREE

REBA flew back to New York in the middle of the following week. Those few days with her family had been a strain, but somehow she had managed to get through them without breaking down. That first evening at home she had cried long into the night, her tears muffled by her pillow, but it had been the last time. Afterwards she told herself firmly that there was nothing to gain from thinking it could have been different, that Eliot was the wrong man. What was done was over, and now Eliot was the only man.

Which was why she didn't waste time unpacking when she returned to her apartment. Instead she took a quick shower and changed into a fashionable suit with a short black skirt and buttercup-yellow jacket. Once again she made up well, needing to mask her vulnerable emotions and give them some necessary protection. A dash of perfume, and she was ready to go and search out Eliot, knowing that the sooner this was over the better. She had to be honest with him about her mother, for which she had permission now that they were to be family.

As expected, he was in his office at the family's flagship hotel. He wasn't expecting her, but the pleasure on his face when he saw her walk in warmed her aching spirit.

'Hello, Eliot. I hope I'm not disturbing you,' she apologised, closing the door behind her and advancing into the wood-panelled office.

He met her halfway. 'You have my permission to disturb me any time you like, sweetheart. I'm always happy to see you, you know that. God, you look so beautiful, I'm just going to have to kiss you!' he declared, and proceeded to do just that. Reba returned the kiss more warmly than she ever had, making a statement he wasn't sure he understood, from the way he frowned down at her when he raised his head again. 'Reba?'

She laughed, but it was off-key. 'Yes, Eliot. I came home early to give you my answer, and the answer is yes, I will marry you.'

Uncertainty turned to joy, and he swept her back into his arms, hugging her almost breathless. 'You'll never regret it, sweetheart, never. I know you don't love me, but you will. I'm going to love you so much that you won't be able to help yourself!'

Reba's hands clutched at the fine material of his jacket, laughing a little desperately as her eyes misted. 'Oh yes, Eliot, do that! And I promise I'll make you a good wife. We'll be happy, won't we?' It was a cry from the depths of her despairing heart.

'Ecstatically happy,' he agreed as he released her and, with the eagerness of a small boy, crossed to his desk and buzzed his secretary. 'Hilary, get them to send up a bottle of the finest champagne and two glasses, will you? And while you're about it, ring my jeweller and have them bring round a selection of engagement-rings. Reba has just agreed to marry me.'

Reba didn't hear what Hilary said, but it obviously pleased Eliot, for he laughed and rubbed his hands. Shaking his head and grinning, he stood and stared at her as if unable to believe his luck.

'You realise she'll spread it all around the building?' she said wryly. It was done now, a fact, and soon everyone would know. There was no turning back.

'Who cares? I'm the happiest man alive right now, and I want everyone to know it!' he declared, then sobered a little. 'Come to think of it, I'd better tell my family soon. There will be hell to pay if they hear it through the jungle-drums first. What about your family? You can ring them from here if you like.'

This was the awkward moment Reba had been anticipating, and she licked her lips, rubbing her hands along her skirt nervously. 'They already know. I had to go home to England first, because my mother was taken ill.'

Eliot was by her side in a second, urging her towards a leather couch and sitting down beside her. 'Nothing serious, I hope?'

'Actually it is serious. We've known for a long time that she has to have an urgent operation. The only hospital which can perform it is over here, and, as you can imagine, it's going to cost the earth. That's why I take every job offered me. I'm saving up to pay for it.' As she reached the end of her explanation, she stared at her tensely interlaced fingers and waited.

'Saving up could take you forever! Why on earth didn't you come and ask me for the money?' he asked, just as she had known he would.

She looked up at him with a sigh. 'Oh, Eliot, I couldn't just come and ask for that kind of money! Besides, my mother wouldn't accept it.'

'Stupid. Your mother doesn't have to know. Now, I don't want any argument from you, Reba. The money is yours. Just let me know when you need to pay, and I'll write out a cheque. I don't care what you tell your mother, but the truth will be our secret, right?'

There was an infinitesimal moment then when she longed to refuse, but there was no way back. This, after all, was what it had all been about. 'If I accept, it's on the understanding that I pay you back,' she argued.

Eliot smiled broadly. 'Anything you say, sweetheart, anything you say,' he conceded, just as there was a knock on the door and Hilary came in with a tray carrying the champagne and two glasses.

'Congratulations, Mr Thorson, Miss Wyeth. I hope you'll be very happy,' the secretary greeted them, smiling warmly. 'Oh, and the jewellers say they'll be here shortly,' she added before leaving.

Reba watched Eliot pour the champagne, knowing she had won a moral victory. She *would* pay him back. It was the only way she could feel comfortable with herself. And she would make him a good wife, so that he would never regret asking her.

He returned to sit beside her, handing her her glass and chinking it against his. 'To us,' he proposed, and Reba forced her lips to smile back.

'To us,' she echoed, and drank a desperate measure, hoping that Eliot was so caught up in his own happiness that he wouldn't see how fragile she was.

Sitting back he put an arm about her shoulders and eased her up against him. 'I don't know about you, sweetheart, but I don't want to wait any longer than I have to to get married.'

She whole-heartedly agreed with that. There was nothing to be gained by waiting, save more doubts, and she had enough of those already. 'The sooner the better, as far as I'm concerned.'

'Great. The way I see it, if your mother has to come over here anyway, we can get married Stateside. What about your family, though? Would you have many relatives who have to be invited?'

'There's only the four of us. Both our parents were only children, and if we have any other relatives, we can't be on speaking terms with them.'

'Lucky you! The Thorson clan would fill a small stadium, and the worst of it is, you can't ignore any of them. They'd be insulted if they weren't invited.' Despite his words, he sounded amused, but she didn't miss the abrupt sobering of his smile before he went on. 'Speaking of which, I expect that means I'll have to invite Hunter.'

The name tore through Reba like a blunt sword, setting every nerve twanging. She had to have heard wrong, she tried to convince herself, and even if she hadn't, it meant nothing. It wasn't an uncommon name, and men frequently referred to each other by surname, didn't they? And yet, what if...? She had to know. Had to learn if her fears were groundless or had foundation.

'Invite who?' Her voice was little more than a croak, and she swallowed some more champagne to moisten her tight throat.

'Hunter Jamieson, my cousin. You don't know him. We don't exactly hit it off, but he's a case in point. He's part of the family, so he'll have to be invited. Mind you, if he had any decency he'd decline,' he retorted, clearly without much hope of that happening.

Her mind began to work furiously. The name was the same, but there had to be some mistake. Her Hunter couldn't possibly be related to the wealthy Thorsons. Once again she had to know. 'Actually, the name does sound rather familiar,' she ventured. 'What does he do?'

Eliot snorted. 'He'd call it messing about with boats, but that's just his little joke. He designs and builds boats for his living.'

His little joke! Reba stared down blindly into her glass. There was no mistake, and the true horror of it finally struck her. Hunter was Eliot's cousin! Dear God, they would be related! After all she had done to put him from her life, she was about to marry his cousin! Hysteria bubbled up inside her, and she forced it back. She mustn't lose her grip now. Eliot said they didn't get on. Perhaps that meant they never met. After all, a man who built boats was a far cry from one who ran a chain of hotels!

Her heart was thundering in her chest as she probed the full extent of the damage. 'Do you see much of him?'

Eliot scowled. 'Too much! He's got shares in the hotels and sits on several boards. Which means he has to be entertained because he's too damned influential to ignore! You've probably heard of Backbay Marine? Well, he inherited that from his father and turned it into the multimillion-dollar business it is now. He's not the kind of relative you can ignore publicly, even if you do so privately.'

Multimillion-dollar business! Reba began to laugh. It was either that or scream. Hunter the deck-hand turned out to be Hunter the astute businessman! A man who, loving her as he had, would have helped her. She had always known that, but she hadn't thought he had the means to do so. That was why she had turned him against her. Made him hate her and think her a gold-digger. Now she knew differently, but it wouldn't change what he thought. If she went to him now, he would believe it was because she had found out about his wealth and only wanted him for his money.

Dear God, why hadn't he told her who he was before she had destroyed everything? Why had he lied?

The heart-broken questions were obsolete even before they were raised. What difference did it make? She *had* destroyed them. More than that, she had given Eliot her promise to marry him. She couldn't go back on her word. There was still her mother to think of. Though it hurt to the very depths of her soul to know she had lost Hunter for nothing, she had to make the best of what she had now. She didn't know how she would face Hunter when the time came, but prayed for the courage to do so. She would pray also for the strength to face his presence on the edge of her life, a constant reminder of what might have been.

'Sweetheart, are you all right?' Eliot's concerned question brought her from the edge of the pit, sobering her at once.

'I'm sorry, I think it's the champagne. I've been so worried about Mum that my nerves are on edge,' she invented swiftly, amazed at how easily the lies came.

He immediately took her glass away. 'Then you'd better not have any more. And don't let my talk about Hunter upset you. He doesn't mean anything to us. We don't need his permission to be happy.'

Reba sank back against his shoulder, tired out by how complicated her life had become in such a short time. For her mother's sake she had to pretend to be in love with Eliot, and now she realised how important it was that he should never know that she and Hunter had ever met, let alone been lovers.

'I'm going to take you out tonight for the best meal you've ever had,' Eliot interrupted her thoughts. 'And I've just realised things couldn't have worked out better. I'm supposed to be going down to the island to join Mother for a holiday this weekend. Now we can go together, and I can introduce you to the important members of the family.'

'Lovely,' Reba agreed, desperately trying to inject enthusiasm into her voice. It was going to be all right. Hunter didn't count any more. The problem was, how long would it take her heart to accept it?

At ten-thirty on Friday morning Reba went to answer the ringing of her doorbell. She took a quick glance in the hall mirror as she passed it. Her make-up was flawless and perfectly understated, the pale pink silk blouse and silver-grey trousers comfortable yet elegant. The lush waves of hair flowed around her head and shoulders, and her fingers fluffed it into greater buoyancy. Eliot loved it this way, often stroking its silky texture as if she were the cat her eyes suggested.

Those same eyes glazed over at unbidden recollections of other hands tangling themselves in the vibrancy of her hair. But such thoughts were pointless, and she clamped down on them rigidly, knowing it was self-destructive to keep stirring up this hornets' nest of memories.

She forced herself back to the present. She was engaged to Eliot. The opulent diamond ring which now graced her marriage finger was proof of that. It wasn't the ring she would have chosen for herself, but on Wednesday she hadn't had the strength to argue. Then, yesterday, it had bolstered her to contact both her mother's doctor, and the Chamberlain Hospital, to confirm that the arrangements for the operation could now be made without delay. It had helped, too, when she had telephoned home and, during a long chat with her mother, had had to reaffirm her love for Eliot. The lack of strength in Harriet Wyeth's voice witnessed her declining health, and Reba was all the more certain that she was doing the right thing.

Satisfied with the way she looked, she passed on to open the door, knowing it would be Eliot on the other side. Her smile of welcome was genuine as she beheld him. She really did like him a lot. She just hoped it would be enough. Today he looked extremely handsome in a lightweight grey suit and striped shirt.

'Hello, sweetheart,' he declared huskily as he drew her into his arms. Reba obediently raised her lips to accept his long kiss. It was nice being in his arms, she told herself, and she always enjoyed his kisses. So what if her pulse didn't race and her blood didn't zing through her veins? They were symptoms of desire, not happiness, and she didn't need the one for the other. Yet she returned his kiss with more than usual enthusiasm because her conscience was pricking her.

'I'm sorry about last night,' she said contritely, when at last she was free to do so, allowing her head to rest briefly on his shoulder as he steered them inside and closed the door. Eliot had wanted to spend the night with her, but she hadn't felt able to take her commitment that far. He had taken her refusal well, but she had still felt guilty. She had told herself that it was because it was too soon. That it would be different when they were married. She had to believe that.

'I'm sorry too. I shouldn't have pressured you like that. It's just that I love you so much, Reba,' Eliot responded, and Reba heard the persuasion in his voice. It made her tense up, and she eased herself away to frown up at him.

'You agreed to wait until we were married,' she reminded him. Maybe she wasn't doing herself any favours, but she only knew that she didn't want to cross that final barrier until she had to, because then the past would really be over.

Eliot groaned. 'I know I did, but I wouldn't be human if I didn't try to change your mind now and then, would I?'

Of course he wouldn't. He was a man, with a man's needs, and he loved her. Reba slipped her arms around him and sighed. How could she tell him she only wanted one man, and he was lost to her? How to tell him she was prepared to honour her commitment, but not just yet? It was just too soon, that was all. When the time came, it would be all right. Until then, she continued her white lie. 'I'm sorry, Eliot, but it means a lot to me to wait, and it won't be much longer,' she promised.

Hugging her closer, he buried his face against her neck. 'Lord, I hope not, but you haven't seen the Thorson machine go into action over a wedding! The planning alone will take a month!'

Reba hated herself for feeling relieved, but there was no denying it. What on earth was she hoping time would bring, a miracle? A reprieve? Damn it, she had chosen. Now she had to get on with her life!

'I was thinking of a wedding in two weeks, three at the most.'

Eliot eased her away to arm's length and smiled ruefully. 'I'm afraid the Thorson name requires that everything should be done correctly. There can be no such thing as a quickie wedding; we have too much regard for our dignity,' he intoned, tongue in cheek, although she suspected there was more than a grain of truth in it.

Nonetheless Reba smiled. 'There are some who would say that's a rather antiquated idea.'

Eliot grinned, slipping a casual arm about her shoulders. 'Of course, and I'm one of them, but it wouldn't do to offend the old folks. Mother is head of the family, and she insists we all have a proper consideration for who we are,' he told her consolingly. 'As the future Mrs Thorson, you'd better get prepared to uphold the family traditions, and pass them on to our children. Which I know you'll manage superbly. And by the way, you look stunning. Good enough to eat. The family will most definitely approve.'

Reba laughed and punched his shoulder playfully. 'Don't try to scare me by making your mother out to be a monster. I'm marrying you, not your family,' she contested.

'Sorry, sweetheart, but when you get me, you get the whole family,' he teased.

Hunter too? The thought came unbidden, and twisted her up inside so that for a moment she felt sick. When she had learnt of the relationship, her peace had gone. The prospect of constantly running into Hunter had shattered her. It was going to be a punishment from which there would be no reprieve.

'Why don't we just elope, and tell them all about it afterwards?' she suggested, perfectly serious. Anything to miss the family gathering which loomed threateningly on the horizon.

Eliot burst out laughing and hugged her again. 'That's what I adore about you, Reba, your sense of humour. Besides, look at it this way: your mother should be well on the road to recovery by then, and much more able to attend the wedding. You'd want that, wouldn't you?'

Reba reached up to cup his face. 'You know, when you say things like that, I know I made the right decision,' she said huskily, knowing he'd never guess that the moisture in her eyes was due to what she had lost, not what she had.

He sent her a tender smile, and kissed her deeply. 'I'm glad,' he said gruffly, before adroitly changing the subject. 'So, are you all packed? Our flight leaves in two hours, and the traffic is bad today. I want us to make a good impression, so it wouldn't do to be late for dinner.'

Reba laughed teasingly. 'That would never do!'

'I've changed my mind—my family aren't going to like you, they're going to love you. Just as I do, darling.'

'I hope you're right,' she murmured, pointing to where her cases stood beside the couch. There was enough against them without having to fight his close family too. But she had to think positively, because it was too late for anything else. Collecting her jacket and purse, she shut the door firmly on her fears and followed him out into the corridor.

When they approached it at last, after hours of energy-sapping travel, the sun was already setting over the surprisingly substantial Caribbean island belonging to the Thorson family. It was a breathtaking sight, indescribable and yet unforgettable, and, in Reba's opinion, quite made up for a long delay earlier, when they had had to wait for the boat.

She would have called Eliot up to share her enjoyment, but he had turned out to be a poor sailor, turning green at the slightest motion. He had finally gone below to get a drink and lie down, refusing her offer to keep him company. She had preferred to stay topside, where the cooling breeze had been welcome. All the way south the temperature had been rising, and at times it had bordered on the unbearable. There was a feeling in the air of something explosive waiting to happen.

Reba sighed, and lifted the weight of her hair off her neck, shivering a little as the breeze touched her damp flesh. Perhaps her unease was due to being back among the islands where she had met Hunter. It helped to know he had already left, and, if he ran a business, that surely meant he wasn't likely to return south so soon. Moreover, she was going to a private island where he simply wouldn't be invited. That should give her a measure of confidence.

The sound of footsteps made her turn to see Eliot coming towards her. The green tinge had gone, and she smiled sympathetically. 'Feeling better?'

Tossing aside the jacket he had been carrying, he slipped his arms around her waist. 'Much, now I can see the end is in sight,' he rejoined wryly.

She sent him a puzzled look. 'Why on earth do you own a yacht if you get seasick?'

'I use it for entertaining, not to sail on. I only travel on water when I have to, like now. What do you think of our little island?'

She sank back against him, her hands coming to rest on his bare arms. 'It's beautiful,' she pronounced honestly. Even from this distance, it looked like a corner of paradise to her. 'But I'd hardly call it little!'

Eliot gave a wry chuckle. 'Well, that depends on your point of view, darling. As a nation we tend to think big, so anything which isn't huge must be small.'

'You own it all?' she asked, suddenly wondering how she would fit into a family who were wealthy enough to own a whole island.

It had seemed a reasonable question to ask, and she was surprised at the sudden tension which went through him.

'Not quite,' he replied tersely, releasing her and coming to stand by her side, hands curled tightly around the rail. Reba realised she had unwittingly touched on a sore point. 'We used to, but now the south-west corner belongs to...someone else.'

He made it sound so dire that she couldn't help being intrigued. 'How come?'

'A whim of my grandfather's. It's a sore point with Mother, so don't mention I told you,' Eliot pronounced grimly.

Protectively she brought her hand up to shade her eyes as she stared ahead. 'If you don't want him there, can't you buy him out?'

When he laughed, it wasn't a particularly pleasant sound. 'Do you think we haven't tried? The bastard won't sell. He enjoys being a thorn in our side.'

She shivered, wondering just who this stranger was who could make her easygoing Eliot sound so bitter. Yet she refused to let it put a cloud on the day. She concentrated instead on the approaching island. It still shimmered in the heat, almost assuming a mirage effect. But through the haze she could see golden tropical beaches and lush greenery. Towards one end hills rose in stately splendour, and straight ahead, beside a small collection of buildings, a sturdy jetty jutted out into the sparkling sea.

'Who lives there?' Reba asked, noting that their arrival had brought several children out on to the jetty, to stand waving. Laughing with real pleasure, she smiled and waved back.

'You shouldn't encourage them, darling. They're damn nuisances, and we'll only have them hanging round us all the time,' Eliot complained.

'But they're only children,' she protested, finding it impossible not to respond to the smiling faces she gradually distinguished as they drew closer to shore. 'Who do they belong to?'

'They're the servants' children. Those are their houses you can see. We find it's more convenient if they don't all live in, especially as the house is shut up for so many months. Lord knows what they'd get up to if we let them have the run of the place. They have some land on which to grow their own crops, and boats to get to the other islands. They're perfectly happy,' Eliot observed, but Reba, shocked to hear such a colonial attitude in the nineties, couldn't help wondering if that was the servants' opinion too.

By the time they docked, several adults had joined the group—cheerful islanders in colourful clothes, who willingly reached down hands to help her alight. Reba barely had time to thank them before she was surrounded by tiny figures. She adored children, wanting to have several of her own, and would have liked to make friends with these, but Eliot was by her side in an instant, shooing them away.

'Bye. See you soon,' Reba called after them, and received large grins and waves for her trouble.

Eliot wasn't best pleased. 'For goodness sake, Reba, you sound just like Hunter. He'd be playing games with them!'

Secretly she was pleased to hear it. She had always felt that Hunter would make a good father. Eliot, on the other hand... 'I thought you wanted children?'

'I do, but not little savages like these. Ours will be properly brought up.' He dismissed the subject tersely, and, taking her arm, led her to where a gleaming automobile stood waiting in the shade.

Reba thought it did children good to act like little savages sometimes, though that wasn't how she would have described the island children. When they had their own family, she was going to make sure their natural enthusiasm wasn't repressed.

'Damn it, where's Vincent?' Eliot's petulant demand drew her attention back to the present.

'Who?'

'The chauffeur,' Eliot explained crossly. 'He should be with the car.'

One of the men loading their luggage into the back of the vehicle looked round. 'Vincent's gone to the mainland, boss. Miz Thorson said for you to drive yourself up to the house.'

'Oh, great!' Eliot exploded, and, muttering under his breath, he settled Reba into the passenger seat before climbing in behind the wheel.

Attempting to pour oil on troubled waters, Reba placed her hand on his arm. 'Never mind, it can't be a long drive on an island this size.'

Eliot sent her a scowl. 'It's not the length of the journey, Reba. I don't pay someone to drive me only to have to do it myself!'

Reba stared at him with raised brows. 'I suppose you can dress yourself and tie your own shoelaces?' she asked in irritation, because he had done nothing but gripe since they landed. Surprised, he blinked twice before visibly relaxing and smiling.

'You think I'm being childish and overreacting?'

Relenting, she tipped her head consideringly. 'Just a bit,' she agreed, and he sighed and started the car.

'You're right. I'm sorry,' he apologised, setting them moving, but she noted he didn't think of apologising to the people he had spoken to so sharply.

This was the difference in their upbringing and, although she didn't like it, she knew she would have to get used to it, until she could bring about some changes. That gave an extra sense of purpose to her marriage. Eliot wasn't the type to be deliberately unkind; he simply had never given thought to what he did.

Five minutes later he brought the car to a sliding halt and, while Reba looked on in mystification, reached into the rear seat for his jacket. From an inside pocket he produced a gift-wrapped package.

'This is for you.'

Since their engagement, she had found it difficult to refuse the presents he kept giving her. She didn't need them, and they made her feel uncomfortable. Still, she produced a smile, because she knew he enjoyed giving her things. 'You're spoiling me,' she protested, even as her fingers reluctantly picked at the wrapping, uncovering a long thin box which she snapped open to reveal a diamond-encrusted watch. 'Oh, Eliot!' she gasped, stunned into speechlessness.

While she looked on, he quickly removed her old watch from her wrist and put the new one in its place. 'Like it?' he queried lightly, but his eyes were intense.

I'm really not cut out for this, she thought helplessly. Why can't I accept it and not feel cheap because I know I don't love him? Other women would. She'd just have to make him happy, and showing pleasure would do that. She raised misty golden eyes to his and smiled.

'I love it! Thank you, darling,' she said gruffly, closing the gap between them to brush her lips over his. But when she would have moved away, Eliot's hand came up behind her head, holding her there while he deepened the kiss searchingly.

When he finally released her, it was only to arm's length, as if he couldn't bear to let her go further. 'Mmm... I needed that. Do you know why I always bring you presents, Reba?'

Lord, how she wished he would just restart the car and drive on. 'Because you're the most generous man I know?'

'Generosity has nothing to do with it. I buy you gifts because I love seeing your face light up when I give them to you,' he told her fervently.

Reba sighed, caught out by her own acting ability. 'I know you like giving me gifts, but you really don't have to,' she proclaimed huskily.

Eliot let his eyes rove over her. 'You're so cool and beautiful, so elegant and aloof. I can't believe my luck in winning you. Darling, I'm so crazy in love with you, I dread the thought of losing you.'

For a moment she thought she might break into hysterical laughter, but a deep breath held it back. 'You don't have to buy me things to keep me, Eliot. I gave you my promise to marry you, and I'm not going to go back on it.'

He laughed then, a confident sound, and reached out to restart the engine. 'I know, but I won't feel totally secure until I'm walking back down the aisle with you on my arm.'

As the car began to move again Reba sank back into her seat, turning her head away from him so that he shouldn't see the bleakness in her eyes as his words conjured up another vision, another face. 'You'll never lose me, Eliot.' You're all I have now. All I have.

CHAPTER FOUR

REBA'S first thought, when she entered the lounge on Eliot's arm before dinner, was that Mrs Thorson was the archetypal matriarch. Elegantly coiffured and dressed, despite the humidity, she looked handsomely regal and remote. Sensing critical eyes surveying her, Reba was glad of her choice of evening-wear. The black sheath dress was an original, and although it clung to her slender curves lovingly it ended a few inches below her knees. She hoped there was nothing there to affront Thorson sensibilities, especially as she wanted to make a good impression.

However, there was more to Mrs Thorson than met the eye, for her face broke into a charming smile as she held her hands out to her son.

'Eliot!'

There was genuine affection in her tone, and Reba felt her own nervous tension ease slightly. She stood back while mother and son embraced, then stepped forward when he beckoned her.

'Darling, let me introduce you to my mother.'

'I'm pleased to meet you, Mrs Thorson,' she greeted politely, and received a gracious smile in return.

'So you're the young woman my son tells me he's going to marry. You must forgive me for sounding a little surprised, Miss Wyeth, but we knew nothing about you until Eliot telephoned yesterday to say he was bringing you with him,' Mrs Thorson explained after they had shaken hands.

64

Of course, that would explain why Eliot had been acting a little out of character. This was a big moment for him, and naturally he wanted his family's approval of his choice. Slipping her hand through his arm, she sent him an encouraging smile.

'Please, call me Reba, Mrs Thorson. I hope, once you've got over the shock, that we can be friends,' she invited sincerely.

His mother smiled again. 'Oh, I'm sure we shall. Now, don't stand on ceremony. You must make yourself quite at home here.'

Eliot, looking extremely handsome in a dinner-jacket which fitted him perfectly, gave an audible sigh of relief. 'Didn't I tell you how beautiful she is, Mother?' he challenged proudly.

Mrs Thorson patted his cheek and smiled. 'She's very lovely, Eliot. Now, why don't you pour us all a glass of sherry, there's a dear boy?' she suggested, cleverly disguising what was, in fact, an order.

Having watched him obey her command, the older woman turned to Reba with a conspiratorial smile. 'I always like a small sherry before dinner, but really that was just an excuse for us to have a little privacy. He won't let you out of his sight otherwise. Now, please don't take this amiss, my dear, but I hope you won't rush into anything. I've always considered the formal period of an engagement to be an admirable idea, because it gives one the chance to realise one's mistakes before any irreparable damage has been done. Marriages are less painful to get into than out of.'

Reba appreciated Mrs Thorson's concern. When she became a mother, she knew she would probably feel the same. 'Common sense doesn't offend me, Mrs Thorson,' she responded lightly, and the older woman relaxed.

'You're sensible. I like that. Have you known my son long?'

'Several months. Long enough to know we can be happy together.'

Mrs Thorson took that in her stride, replying with a sortie of her own. 'And what do your own parents say?'

Reba had to smile, realising it was possible to like this woman after all. 'My father died when I was young, but my mother was thrilled. She just wants me to be happy.' The words brought an ache to her heart, and she forced herself to ignore it. She *would* be happy. 'Eliot and I are both adults, Mrs Thorson, and I'm sure you understand why we don't see the point of waiting any longer than we have to.'

Mrs Thorson nodded sympathetically. 'Of course. I expect I understand more than you think I do.' For a moment she sounded grim, but when she looked at Reba her expression was amused. 'After all, I was young once myself. Ah, I don't believe you've met my daughter, Eleanor,' she continued smoothly, indicating a young woman who had just entered the room.

Eleanor Thorson could have been her brother's twin, but was in fact several years younger. She was extremely pretty, but right now there was a tight look about her mouth, and her smile didn't reach her eyes. When she shook hands, Reba could actually feel the tension in her.

'Eliot said you were a model,' his sister ventured tautly, not glancing at her mother.

Something was wrong, and Reba flashed her a friendly smile, trying to put her at ease. 'That's correct.'

Eleanor responded with a fleeting smile. 'I wanted to be a model once, but I stopped growing!' she said ruefully.

Reba laughed in commiseration. 'You do have to be tall, I'm afraid. But don't be too upset. It isn't as glamorous as you think. A lot of the time it's hard work for very little money. You'd be better off doing something else.'

For a moment Eleanor allowed herself to relax. 'That's what I told myself. Now I'm studying art history instead. Mother does not approve!' She said it with a fond glance at her parent, so Reba knew that wasn't the cause of her inner tension.

Mrs Thorson tutted. 'I refuse to be drawn tonight, Eleanor. Go and see if Eliot needs a hand,' she advised, before turning to Reba with a heartfelt sigh. 'Shall we sit down?' She indicated the couch behind them. 'Reba— such an interesting name. I don't believe I've ever come across it before. Is it your own, or a professional one?'

That prompted a discussion about her career and her family which lasted until dinner was announced. The meal was a delight on two fronts. Not only was the food beautifully prepared, but Mrs Thorson was an accomplished hostess, and she cleverly kept the conversational ball moving. Even Eleanor remained relaxed, although she began to show signs of tension again towards the end.

By then Reba was certain she had made a good impression, and Eliot seemed to think so too, for he reached out to squeeze her hand. 'What did I tell you, darling? How could Mother fail to like you?' he pronounced softly.

She smiled. 'I like her too.'

Across the table, Eleanor cleared her throat. 'Oh, by the way, Mother, I meant to tell you earlier, I've invited Sibyl to join us tomorrow,' she declared brusquely, drawing everyone's attention.

Reba winced as Eliot's fingers tightened about hers, but it didn't stop her noticing the younger woman was braced for trouble. This explained her earlier behaviour, and she tensed in silent support.

Mrs Thorson raised a hand to her throat. 'Really, Eleanor!' she said faintly, eyes turning rather anxiously to her son.

That exchange of glances sent a finger of unease down Reba's spine. 'Who is Sibyl?' she asked, and for a moment it seemed she wasn't going to receive an answer.

'Sibyl Haggerty,' his sister eventually explained, taking the bull by the horns. 'We were at school together. She's been away in Europe and has only recently come back. I invited her over so we could catch up on all the gossip.'

Reba didn't believe it, and neither did anyone else, although they reacted differently.

Eliot relaxed again, smiling at his sister. 'Naturally, you would. But it wasn't a very kind thing to do when you know Sib and I don't get on,' he pointed out smoothly.

Eleanor jutted out her chin, eyes accusing. 'You used to.'

'But not any more. Ring her and tell her to come another time,' Eliot ordered, but his sister shook her head mutinously.

'I will not!'

'That will do!' Mrs Thorson intervened sternly. She sounded calm, but her fingers were crumpling her napkin. 'If Eleanor has invited Sibyl, then we must make her welcome. I will expect everyone to be on their best behaviour.' Was it a coincidence that her eyes were on her son as she said that? 'Now, if you'll oblige me by ringing for Neville, Eliot, he'll bring the champagne I had put on ice in order to toast you and Reba.'

Eliot looked as if he might refuse, but then he released Reba's hand, allowing her to rub it and restore the blood-flow. She watched as he rose and went to the bell. What on earth had that been all about? This Sibyl was clearly a bone of contention between brother and sister, and Eleanor wanted to score points. But why? What had Sibyl Haggerty done?

It was a puzzle which she put to the back of her mind as the champagne was poured. Mrs Thorson proposed the toast, and it was while they were drinking it that Reba experienced the overwhelming sensation of being watched. The sensitive hairs all over her body rose to attention, and her head came up abruptly, her golden eyes meeting and locking on to a pair of deep blue ones. Eyes which could plumb the depth and breadth of her soul.

Hunter! All the air seemed to leave her body in a rush.

He stood on the terrace, just outside the French doors which had been left open to allow in whatever breeze there was to cool them. He looked much as he had done the very first time she had seen him, down to the white vest and faded, torn jeans which clung to every muscle. He was a potent presence which she could never forget, and her body responded on a primitive level. Oh God, she could have been given a hundred years to prepare for this meeting, and it would not have been enough. The source of all her happiness and all her pain stood before her, and she could not have moved or spoken if her life had depended upon it, such was his effect upon her.

Yet her brain pounded out questions. What was he doing here? What did it mean? Had he followed her? Dear God, what was he going to do? That last question exploded in her brain as she was made painfully aware that he held immense power. She had been so worried about seeing him again, when her defences were so weak, that she had missed the fact that he had the power to destroy everything!

'Reba? Honey, are you all right?' Eliot's concerned voice seemed to come from a long way away, but it broke the spell, and she dragged in a painful breath as a sheen of perspiration broke out on her forehead.

She didn't have to reply, for the silent man at the window moved and drew everyone's attention. There was a moment of absolute stillness as he stepped inside into the light, then Eliot shot to his feet, his glass toppling off the table to crash to the floor unnoticed.

'What the hell are you doing here, Hunter?' he demanded angrily, much to his cousin's amusement.

Hunter was perfectly relaxed. Taking his weight on one leg, the other bent in a purely male stance, he crossed his arms over his chest. 'I heard you were welcoming a new member into the family,' he drawled, in a voice which was laced with cynical amusement and succeeded in touching a nerve in Reba which made her shiver. Her fear grew. What was he going to do? Those eyes swivelled to her, not missing the tell-tale swiftness of her breathing. He knew what she was thinking. He was enjoying watching her squirm as she waited for the axe to fall. A few simple words would be all it took. She closed her eyes.

'This her?' she heard him ask, and her lids shot up so that she could stare at his mocking eyes. It was there for her to see. He was going to say nothing—not yet. He had other plans. Like a cat with a mouse, he was going to toy with her before he ended it. And he *would* end it—in his own time.

Eliot's hands clenched into fists. 'You stay away from Reba! You hear me, Hunter?'

Briefly Hunter switched his glance to the other man, and she could breathe again. 'Oh, I hear you fine, cousin,' he confirmed, totally unimpressed, eyes drifting back across the table. 'Reba? Now that's a name which reeks of hot blood and passion. And those eyes! Man, couldn't you just drown in them?'

Already it was beginning, and Reba's soul cried out in agony as his words bombarded her. Things he had said with love were now used to wound. He was deliberately tormenting her. The way he said her name, and the way he looked at her, invited her to remember, and he was so attuned to her that he knew her skin prickled with that awareness she couldn't hide. She wanted to cry out, do something, but all she could do was stare helplessly as he began to cross the room towards her.

Mrs Thorson suddenly found her voice, although it wavered in a fashion Reba would not have believed. 'Hunter, you are not welcome in this house!'

He laughed, and there was something pitying in the look he sent her. 'Don't I know it, Aunt Helena? Rest assured, I'll be going just as soon as I've greeted my new cousin.'

Reba couldn't believe he was doing this. Before them all he was taking a revenge they knew nothing about, and she could do nothing, for fear of betraying herself. He knew it, and he used it. Not words now, but elemental responses. She felt her body absorb the wave of heat which came from his as he reached her side and bent down towards her. A tiny whimper of something which she recognised as fear lodged in her throat. Eyes with impossibly long lashes and rays of tiny laughter lines bored into hers. 'Welcome to the family, Reba,' he intoned huskily, and, before she could make a move to avoid him, his mouth lowered to hers.

Though she fought not to, she closed her eyes as, with incredible arrogance, he plundered her lips. This was no searching out; he knew the moist trail of his tongue over her lips would make her gasp, and when she did, his tongue slid between them, stroking erotically for what seemed endless moments. A frisson of emotion shot through her system, lighting it up. Then it was over. He removed his lips and straightened up, leaving her bereft. Her lids seemed weighted when she lifted them, and then she wished she hadn't when she saw the look in his eyes. It sent the colour rushing from her cheeks, and made him laugh.

Eliot's hand on his shoulder swung him round. 'You bastard. I ought to knock you down for that!' he shouted, his face mottled with angry heat.

Hunter's brows lifted scornfully. With perfect ease he removed the hand from his shoulder and dropped it away. 'Try it, if you think you can.'

Reba's golden eyes widened in alarm at the thought that they might be going to fight, and she knew she had to stop it. She couldn't allow Hunter to hurt Eliot for something she had done. From somewhere she found the strength to get to her feet. Breathing as if she had been in a gruelling race, she placed herself in front of Eliot.

'Leave him alone!'

Hunter allowed himself the luxury of running his shocking gaze down the length of her and up again. 'How touching. You must love him a lot to rush to his defence.'

She winced, knowing the words were a deliberate taunt. He doubted her, and he was right, but for the wrong reasons. But she had made her choice, and must defend it. Her chin lifted. 'Get out!'

He didn't say anything; he didn't have to. The inclination of his head said he was going because he chose to go, not because she ordered it. With that gracefully lazy stride, he headed for the terrace again. In the opening he stopped briefly, his expression serious as he looked at his aunt. 'Thought I'd let you know there's a storm brewing. Be here in a few days, and it's going to be bad. If you need any help, you know where I am.'

Mrs Thorson had regained her poise. 'Thank you, Hunter, but I'm sure we can manage.'

He shrugged, as if he had expected no other response. 'The offer's still there. Goodnight.' He allowed himself a glance round the small tableau. When he found Reba, he raised his finger in salute. 'Reba.' Her name was a husky undertone, and then he was gone.

With his departure the awful tension left the room. Just as suddenly the strength went out of Reba's legs, and she would have fallen if Eliot hadn't been there to prevent it.

'Reba, darling, are you all right?' he cried, assisting her to a chair and kneeling beside her anxiously. 'Damn Hunter. I'll kill him if he's hurt you!'

She didn't think she'd ever be all right again. 'He didn't hurt me,' she lied, for he had, so deeply that she knew it would take a long time, if not forever, to recover. She looked up to find herself surrounded. Hysterically she knew she had to say something, and there was only one thing *to* say. She had to keep up the fiction of not knowing him. 'Did you call him Hunter?'

'That's right. Hunter Jamieson is my nephew, and could best be described as the black sheep of the family. He owns property at the other side of the island,' Mrs Thorson informed her in an icy voice. 'I'm sorry you were subjected to his peculiar brand of...humour. He knows he isn't welcome here, but he does things like this to annoy us.'

If there was more to it, and Reba didn't doubt that for a second, she was in no state to hear it. Outwardly she had to look no worse than shaken by the experience, while deep inside she was still reeling. What she really wanted right now was to find a place where she could assimilate the awfulness of what had happened to her tonight. She needed to be by herself.

'I'm sorry, but would you mind if I went to my room?' Her eyes went to the older woman, to find she was already watching her in some concern.

'Not at all, dear. You've had quite a shock. Eliot will take you up.' She watched as he slipped an arm around Reba's waist and helped her to her feet. 'I'll wish you goodnight, Reba. Do try to sleep well. Eliot, I'll see you in the library shortly. We have some talking to do.'

'Very well, Mother,' he acknowledged over his shoulder as they left the room.

Halfway up the grand staircase which swept up from the hall, Reba felt in control enough to ask a much-needed question.

'Hunter's the man you spoke about, isn't he? The one who owns part of the island? Why didn't you tell me?'

Eliot glanced down at her, a nerve ticking away in his jaw. 'I hoped he wouldn't be here. You never know with Hunter; he comes and goes as he pleases. We do our best to ignore him.' His fist thumped the banister rail. 'When I think of him kissing you...!'

Reba's throat closed over. She hadn't been able to stop thinking of him kissing her! 'I'd rather not talk about it.'

'No,' he agreed, seeing her pale face and mistaking the reason for it. 'I was proud of the way you stood up to him, Reba, but you'd better take care to avoid his part of the island. I wouldn't want you to run into him when you're alone.'

He made Hunter sound like some sort of criminal, and she was forced to hold back a sharp retort that he wasn't like that. Oh, tonight he had been cruel, but he had had cause. Usually he was kind and warm and loving. All this she could have said, but she wasn't supposed to know him, and could only steel herself to bear it. It was all part of the tangled web her life had become.

'I don't think he's dangerous,' was all she could say in his defence, and it carried no weight with Eliot.

'No, but you've already seen he's no respecter of property or person.'

By this time they had reached her room, and she opened the door, holding on to the handle, reluctant to have him enter. 'I'm sorry to have spoilt the evening.'

'Hunter did that already,' Eliot pronounced grimly. He took her by the shoulders and would have kissed her lips if she hadn't twisted just enough for him to catch her cheek instead. She didn't want any more kisses to-night. Or, her treacherous heart taunted, didn't she want Eliot's superimposed on that other? However taunting it might have been, it had been Hunter's kiss, and she had never expected to experience it again.

'Goodnight,' she said hoarsely as he released her.

'Poor darling, you're all done in. Damn that man! Somehow he always manages to spoil everything. Sleep well, I'll see you at breakfast.' He turned away and Reba slipped inside her room, closing the door and locking it.

Flicking on the light, she stared at her surroundings without seeing them. Earlier she had found the large bedroom-cum-sitting-room, decorated, like the adjoining bathroom, in shades of cream and the palest of pinks, charming and elegant. But that was before dinner—and Hunter.

Legs still suffering from a betraying tremble took her to the dressing-table where she dropped down on to the stool. The shock when he had walked into the room was still reverberating through her. Reba felt a lump of ice form in her stomach. Hunter owned part of the island! This was a continuing nightmare. Wherever she turned,

Hunter's dark shadow loomed over her. She couldn't even be free of him here.

Her heart was still beating erratically, and she placed a hand on her breast as if to calm it. But even that soft touch brought a gasp as it made contact with tender flesh, and she realised with a shock that her nipple stood in a state of proud arousal.

Slowly her eyes lifted to their own reflection, and read the truth there. Just looking at Hunter had sent a charge of electricity through her system. It was almost funny to realise that everyone else had assumed her shock was for something other than recognition. Hunter had known otherwise; that was why he had chosen to kiss her. At his touch her body had come alive, and he had known it. He knew every inch of her intimately, and every one of her responses. Nothing had changed. Nothing was forgotten... or forgiven. The contempt she had seen in his eyes had told her that.

Jumping to her feet, she paced to the window, resting her flushed cheek against the cool glass. He had taken great delight in taunting her! Daring her to—what? Admit that she knew him? Her hand shot to her throat. She would never do that—but what if *he* did?

Dear God, what if he told Eliot that they had once had an affair?

Surely he wouldn't do that? Or would he—if he hated her enough? The thought made her go cold. She had made him hate her by throwing away his love in her supposed search for wealth. Wouldn't it be poetic justice for him, to cause her to lose Eliot just when she believed she had him?

Hunter had suddenly become dangerous. He was a threat she couldn't afford to ignore. Which meant she had to go and see him, find out what he intended to do. Once, she couldn't have waited to see him, but that was in the past. Now, looking for Hunter, she would not find a man who loved her, but one who hated her.

The sun was already high when Reba woke the following morning. When she tried to move she discovered that the sheet was tangled around her body, as if she had been threshing about in her sleep, and in the recesses of her mind the tendrils of a dream still lingered, taunting her. She couldn't recall a single part of it, but she knew it must have been about Hunter, and it left her restless and uneasy as she climbed from the bed.

The air was heavy and oppressive, and the humidity level well on the way to becoming stifling. She showered, and felt moderately better, yet just moving brought a glow to her skin, negating the effect within minutes. Deciding to wear as little as possible, she donned a brief turquoise cotton halter-top and white Bermuda shorts over her panties. Avoiding make-up, which would only run in this heat, she simply brushed her hair, leaving it to flow loosely around her shoulders. If Hunter was right, and there was a storm coming, she prayed it would break soon, shattering the tension which snagged at her nerves. She paused in the act of slipping her feet into comfortable espadrilles.

Thinking of him brought back the need to see him. She had to go, but what excuse could she give for leaving the party? If she was discovered, she could destroy everything herself, without Hunter having to lift a finger! Yet she had no choice. His silence last night meant nothing. She needed to know what he was going to do.

It was that thought which sat uncomfortably on her shoulder as she went down to join the family for breakfast. However, only Mrs Thorson occupied a seat at the table on the terrace when a maid showed Reba out. Eliot's mother greeted her with a pleasant smile.

'Good morning, Reba. I trust you feel better today?'

'Much better, thank you,' she confirmed, as the older woman put aside the letter she had been reading.

'I'm so glad. I thought a good sleep was better for you than an early breakfast; that's why you weren't disturbed. Do help yourself to croissants or fruit. I'll ring for fresh coffee, unless you would prefer tea?'

'Coffee's fine,' Reba agreed, taking a seat.

'I really cannot apologise enough for Hunter's behaviour last night.'

Reba was unable to stop herself from tensing. 'Please don't let it worry you. I certainly won't,' she lied diplomatically. 'We're hardly likely to meet too often.'

Mrs Thorson smiled wryly. 'You don't know him, my dear. He turns up just to spite us. A most disagreeable young man.'

Once more Reba was plunged into the pretence of not knowing him, even as her heart wanted to protest his aunt's claim. It was hard to bite her tongue, and suddenly she saw the years stretch out ahead of her. Years in which she had to keep up the fiction. How on earth could she do it? Every lie demanded another to back it up. It was an impossible task, and the chances of being found out were so many. To lie cold-bloodedly was one thing, but to lie against her own feelings was a betrayal. Never had her loyalties been so divided, and the chances of discovery so great. But she had no choice. She was in this now, and had to go on. She wouldn't make a mistake, because she simply couldn't afford to.

She reached for a peach from the fruit bowl, biting into it with little relish. Her gaze slipped to the view. The flowers were a riot of exotic colours and scents, bordering a lawn which sloped down towards the trees. Through them, and over them, she could glimpse the sparkling blue waters of the ocean, while the breeze carried with it the rhythmic crash of the waves breaking on to the golden sands. 'You have a marvellous view.'

'Its always been one of my favourites. Eliot's too.'

'He can't still be in bed, surely?' Reba asked, belatedly realising it would be very odd if she didn't make some enquiry about her fiancé.

Mrs Thorson consulted her watch. 'No, dear. He had his breakfast several hours ago now. He'll be well on his way.'

'On his way?' Reba echoed in surprise, the peach halting short of her mouth.

'Forgive me, this was all decided in a rush this morning. He's gone to fetch Sibyl. Eleanor was supposed to go, but unfortunately she has one of her sick headaches. Eliot was the natural choice to go and get her,' Mrs Thorson explained calmly, making room for the maid, who had brought a fresh tray.

Reba forgot about the peach as her mind assimilated the news. 'I thought they didn't get along?' she said, and saw a faint pink wash enter the other woman's cheeks.

'They had a falling-out, that's true. But good manners still exist. Someone had to go and collect her, and my son put his dislike aside, as I expected him to do, and agreed to go. We knew you wouldn't mind,' his mother went on easily, pouring a cup of coffee and holding it out to her.

Reba thought it was too late to mind, even if she did. But she would have liked to be asked. All the same, it gave her the opportunity she had been seeking. Provided she was careful, no one need ever know where she had gone. Taking a deep breath, she reached across to take the cup. 'No, I don't mind,' she responded with a wry smile. 'It will give me a chance to do some exploring on

my own. Eliot doesn't much care for walking,' she added
teasingly.

Mrs Thorson's smile broadened. 'There we are then,
everyone's happy. Sibyl and Eliot will be back in plenty
of time for dinner, and then we can really begin to enjoy
the holiday. It couldn't have worked out better.' She rose
as gracefully as ever, retrieving her letter. 'You must
excuse me now. I have some letters to write. Lunch is
at one—an informal affair for those who want it.'

Reba watched her disappear into the house, and heard
her talking to the housekeeper before silence fell. Her
heart thudded a beat or two faster. She mustn't rush, or
do anything which would make it appear she had somewhere to go. In fact, there was no better time to go in
and make some phone calls: the daily one home to her
mother, and another checking the progress of the hospital arrangements. Yet her mind winged ahead. Hunter
would be expecting her, and somewhere between now
and then she must repair the defences he had breached
so easily last night.

CHAPTER FIVE

HALF an hour later, having decided she had waited long enough, Reba left the house by the front door. She didn't know exactly where Hunter lived, and there was nobody of whom she could safely ask directions. But on an island this size she must surely come across his house, if she kept walking long enough. Taking a deep breath, she headed down the road, which was little more than a track, grateful that it was at least marginally cooler under the trees.

Before very long she reached the fork which led down to the small collection of houses by the jetty. It was well-used, unlike the slightly overgrown one which she now discovered ahead of her. Pressing on, she very soon found that the undergrowth seemed to close in around her. It was hard to remember that human beings lived not very far away. Yet somebody used the track, probably the children. They had the run of the island.

She continued to follow the deteriorating track, which twisted and turned so much that she was completely disorientated, and she was just beginning to think she was on the wrong track altogether when she rounded another bend and came upon a building. It wasn't like those by the jetty, or the white two-storey one she had left earlier. Set at the end of the track, it was little more than a large shack, and looked in dire need of repair. It nestled at the foot of a slope, in the curve of a small cove, and, to Reba's critical eye, looked abandoned.

Her first thought was that Hunter couldn't possibly live here, but she decided she had better go and make

sure. There was a veranda built on to the side facing the
sea, and it groaned pitifully as she stepped up on to it.
Automatically she froze, expecting someone to call out,
then uttered a nervous laugh as she realised how foolish
that was. There was nobody around to hear! Walking
forward, she noticed that the door stood open and, biting
her lip, she went to look inside. The first and only thing
her eye alighted on was a table on which stood a kero-
sene lamp, a half-empty bottle of whisky and a book.
There was probably more to see, but her surprise at
finding signs of habitation was turned to shock when a
voice spoke from behind her.

'Looking for something?' it enquired mockingly, and
Reba screamed.

'You got a good pair of lungs, Reba. Pity there's no
one but me around to hear them,' the same unforgettable voice declared, and in seconds the shock had been
replaced by a tingling awareness as the hairs on the back
of her neck rose.

Knowing whom she would see when she turned didn't
at all prepare her for the sight which met her eyes. Hunter
stood at the foot of the rickety steps, staring up at her.
He wore the same jeans as he had last night, but that
was all. His feet were bare and so was his impressive
chest. There were droplets of moisture on the tanned
expanse of skin, and the slicked-back darkness of his
hair told her he must just have come from a dip in the
sea. The thought didn't help.

'Hunter.' His name was a torture and a delight, hovering between a gasp and a groan. As she had found the
previous night, she couldn't tear her eyes away from him.
Ten days or ten years—he was as necessary to her life
as breathing. Just seeing him brought vivid rainbow hues
to an otherwise colourless existence. Her head might have
given him up, but her heart never could. In that instant

she didn't care that her greatest joy was also her greatest pain. She forgot the most basic rules of self-preservation in the need to assimilate him into her system. Her whole body seemed to be liquefying, weakening her knees and making her heart race—blinding her to reality.

She didn't see that one eyebrow lifted mockingly, or that the curve of his lips as he smiled faintly was cynical. 'You were maybe expecting someone else?' he asked, agilely mounting the steps to stand before her, hands hitched on the low-slung jeans.

His sudden closeness made her throat close over. She suffered a sensory bombardment, as if every nerve she possessed had come alive. She could smell the fresh male scent of him combined with the tangy salt of the sea, could feel the heat coming from him in waves. She wanted nothing so much as to walk into his arms and rest her head on his shoulder. To go home.

Her tongue came out to moisten dry lips so that she could speak. 'I didn't expect to find anybody here,' she denied as firmly as she could.

'Didn't they tell you I live here, tiger-eyes?' he taunted softly, and his breath was a warm caress on her face.

Reba closed her eyes, not wanting him to see her anguish at knowing that her pleasure at seeing him was not returned. Fool! His reaction was exactly as she had expected. She had engineered it. But knowing that didn't help when she was standing here, as unable to retreat as if he actually held her captive in his arms, torn by a longing to close that small gap which stood between them, to seek the comfort only he could provide.

Despairingly aware of how stupidly vulnerable she was making herself, Reba attempted to rally her defences. 'They said...they said you lived on the other side of the island, to the south.'

Her gaze dropped to his mouth as he laughed huskily. At once she recalled every detail of that kiss last night, and it made her lips tingle, as if his had brushed hers again. Dear Lord, did he have any idea what he was doing to her, even though he hadn't touched her? She moaned softly, and her gaze rose to lock with his. His eyes were so blue—so cold! She dragged in a ragged breath as their icy sharpness pierced her heart. Her nerves jolted badly. He knew! He knew exactly what he was doing to her, because he was deliberately making it happen! That was why he had chosen to stand so close to her. Shame curled inside her as she realised what a lovesick fool she was. An open book for him to read any time he wanted to.

'Beauty you may have, but your sense of direction stinks. This *is* south, tiger-eyes. As south as you get on this island before you hit the sea. Surely a sailor like yourself would know that?' Seeing the hot colour storm into her cheeks, he laughed. 'It doesn't matter. I knew you'd make your way here sooner or later.'

The claim sent a flame licking through her. She might have been forced to dance to his tune, but she wouldn't do it without a fight. 'Even you couldn't be that certain!'

His hand came up, and one callused finger traced the line of her lips before his hand moved in a caress across her cheek, gliding into her hair, making her eyes close involuntarily as she leant into that touch. 'I kissed you . . . remember?'

The soft words brought her eyes open with another painful jolt to her nerves. In the same instant the proprietorial nature of his touch did what she had been unable to do, and jerked her out of the trance she had been in. She went hot and cold as she became fully aware of what was going on. He was saying she had come because she couldn't stay away and, by allowing him to

touch her so freely, she had appeared to admit it. Blinded
by love, she had forgotten he despised her. Worse, she
had allowed him to see that she was still attracted to
him.

She stepped away from him abruptly, brought close
to tears by a searing wave of despair. Dear God, what
was she thinking of? How could she have made herself
so vulnerable? Tattered pride came to her rescue, even
though one look at his face told her it was much, much
too late.

The knowledge of her betrayal was there in the way
her voice broke. 'Your arrogance takes my... breath
away! H-How dare you assume that your kisses are ir-
resistible? Let me tell you... something. They're
loathsome. Vile!' she choked out, hating the way the
steady gaze of those blue eyes never wavered. It said,
I've seen you, I know you. I expected this reaction and
discount it. A shiver caught her.

'If it was that loathsome and vile, you should have
fought me off,' Hunter responded pointedly, reminding
her that she had done nothing.

Her head reared back, hot colour staining her cheeks.
'I would have, but you took me by surprise!'

'Really? I find that hard to believe, when you recognised me the second you saw me last night.'

Reba's hand stole to her throat. 'I tell you I was
shocked. I never expected to see you again!' she refuted
instantly, but her back was to the wall, and they both
knew it.

Hunter took a step closer, which had her tensing immediately, but it only made him smile. 'Oh, I know that,
tiger-eyes. I was shocked too. But not so shocked that I
didn't recognise it wasn't horror in your eyes when you
looked at me, but hunger!' he revealed crushingly, and
moved past her into the hut.

Reba swayed, as much relieved as devastated by his claim. She *had* hungered, but not sexually, though, God knew, she wanted him. She had hungered for the love she only felt with him. Hunter hadn't realised. He had only seen the wanting as sexual! Though it brought her feelings down to their lowest level, it gave her back her defences.

'So Cousin El's the sucker you've got your hooks into. Does he know you're only marrying him for his money?' Hunter challenged from inside.

As if she had plunged into ice-water, his words brought her back to the fear which had been her reason for coming here in the first place. She felt as if she was being battered by stormy seas, and her heart lurched. Was that a threat? Her nerves stretched to screaming pitch as she battled on.

'Eliot loves me!'

'He probably thinks so, but does he know you don't love him? Love, as we both know so well, not having a place in your scheme of things.'

That brought back memories so painful that she swayed slightly, and she knew she couldn't possibly handle this right now. 'I'm going. I'm not staying to listen to any more of this!' she shouted back, but had taken no more than a step towards the edge of the veranda when Hunter reappeared, two steaming cups of coffee in his hands.

'Running away, Reba?' he taunted softly. 'Now that really isn't wise. It might just make me do the very thing you don't want me to do.'

She stared at him, eyes huge in her pale face. 'What thing?'

'Tell Eliot that you're the worst kind of gold-digger. I should know, because you played for me once, when you thought I had money,' he pronounced, mouth curving in a lazy smile.

Reba closed her eyes, unable to bear the mockery in his. It hurt to breathe. It hurt unbearably to have to ask the question which had burnt in her brain ever since she had discovered who he was. 'But you did have money. Why didn't you tell me?'

He laughed harshly. 'You didn't seriously expect me to tell you just how wealthy I was, when you'd just got through telling me you were looking for a rich husband, did you?'

Pain seemed to well up inside her, because she couldn't tell him that, if only he had told her, none of this need have happened. 'And the yacht?' Why not hear it all— all her folly?

'I'd sailed it down for a friend, after seeing to some repairs. I knew about letting your agency use it, but I hadn't intended skippering it myself. Something changed my mind,' he finished with heavy irony.

Not something, but someone. Herself. 'I see.'

'Do you?' he asked harshly. 'I'd waited all my life for you, tiger-eyes. I'd been fighting off women who only wanted me for my money ever since I'd started making it. Then you came along, and I believed you were the one woman who loved me for myself. I had a very narrow escape. Had you had the guts to marry me, you would have discovered just who I was, and I would never have known you for what you were, would I?' He held out one of the cups. 'Coffee. You look as if you could use some.'

Her legs felt so weak that it was amazing they still held her upright. She ignored the cup, for there was something more important she needed to know. 'Are you going to do it?'

Blue eyes glittered sardonically. 'Tell Eliot? I haven't made up my mind yet. Perhaps if you stay and talk to me, you can help me decide.'

He knew as well as she did that staying was the very last thing she wanted to do, but that his threat made it impossible for her to do anything else. She reached out to take the cup, with fingers that she hoped he didn't notice were something less than steady.

She cupped her fingers round the chipped enamel, as if trying to draw strength from it. 'I didn't know you were related to Eliot until a few days ago,' she said shortly, needing to break the heavy silence which had fallen.

Hunter laughed, a cynical sound which made her wince inwardly. 'That I believe. If you'd known, you would have chosen a different mark.'

Her eyes flew to his, shooting angry sparks which bounced off him. 'Will you stop saying that? Eliot isn't a mark!'

One eyebrow lifted derisively. 'What is he, then, the love of your life? No, no, silly me, I was forgetting *I* was that!'

Reba drew in a painful breath at the accuracy of his low blow. Inside she wept, because he had never said a cruel word until the day she rejected him. She had wanted him to hate her, but she didn't feel proud of having turned him into the man who stood before her. 'I never wanted to hurt you,' she began huskily, only to be interrupted.

'No, you simply wanted my money. When you discovered I supposedly didn't have any, it made me instantly forgettable,' he sneered, eyes like chips of blue ice.

'That's not true!' Reba protested betrayingly, but he seemed not to notice her slip.

'Funny, but I didn't see you running after me with protestations of undying love! Which was probably just as well, because I wouldn't have believed them then any more than I would now. I told you once you don't know what love is and, judging by this latest encounter, you still don't.'

If his intention had been to hurt her, then he had succeeded. 'You bastard!'

His eyes registered his pleasure at scoring a hit. 'Was I supposed to love you forever, Reba?'

Why not? I'll always love you! The silent declaration was a desperate cry from the heart. She took a shaky breath, knowing she had created a monster which would haunt her for the rest of her life.

She shook her head, striving for a semblance of calm to get her through this torturous ordeal. 'It didn't take you long to get over me!'

The glint in his eye gave her warning that she wouldn't like his answer. 'Perhaps it was something you said, tiger-eyes.'

Her lids dropped. 'You must hate me very much.'

He tipped his head to one side consideringly. 'Hate you? I have too much contempt for you to hate you, Reba,' Hunter decided softly.

Because she suddenly wanted quite badly to cry, Reba raised her chin defiantly. 'So what do you want, revenge?'

Hunter sipped at his coffee before answering. 'I could get that by telling Eliot who and what you are, couldn't I?' he mused, eyes dancing.

Reba gritted her teeth. 'You're enjoying this, aren't you?'

Draining his cup, he set it aside. 'It has its amusing side, I have to admit.'

A flash of anger felt good, temporarily cauterising the wound. 'God, you're impossible! You're going to drag this out as long as you possibly can, aren't you?'

His teeth flashed whitely as he grinned. 'I'm fascinated by the idea of watching a gold-digger squirming on the end of someone else's hook!'

Her free hand curled into an impotent fist as she realised how easy it would be to hate him. Perhaps she'd be better off if she did. Yet she didn't, and battled on as best she knew how. 'I can see why your family don't like you!'

A lazy eyebrow lifted quizzically. 'Their reasons differ from yours, and I doubt very much if they told you why.'

'I can appreciate why they don't much care to talk about you,' she replied tartly, and he laughed. Genuinely, as if the family's reaction just amused him and nothing more.

'That way they can pretend I don't exist, while they think up ways to get rid of me.' Seeing her shocked reaction, he grinned. 'Not permanently, just from the island. I'm too important to them elsewhere.'

In an effort to hide the depth of her reaction, when she had thought for a moment that the Thorsons might do him actual physical harm, Reba looked around her. The obvious signs of dilapidation suddenly gave her the idea of how she could shield herself from the worst of his barbs. He already believed she was after money for pure greed, so why not act unrepentant? It was what he would expect anyway. She might just as well be hanged for a sheep as a lamb.

Her nose wrinkled in distaste. 'You can't really live here. This is worse than a slum!' she said scornfully. It wasn't, not really, but it looked dangerous, and it made her shudder to think of him living in it.

'Beauty is in the eye of the beholder. To me, it's perfect. This is my birthright. I was conceived here, and my grandfather left it to me when he died. He would have left it to my mother, but she died years ago, before my father could make an honest woman of her. That's if he intended to. I always give him the benefit of the doubt. My mother was Eliot's father's sister, and what sticks in their craw is that I was born the wrong side of the blanket. While it's marginally acceptable to have a bastard in the family, they don't want him living right under their noses.'

If he had intended to shock her with the confession about his illegitimacy, then he was way off beam. It was on the tip of her tongue to tell him it made no difference to her, when she realised he wouldn't want to know. So she said instead, 'Perhaps they wouldn't mind so much if you did something about this place.'

'You mean, made it more like that colonial monstrosity they live in? Oh no, this suits me fine. Besides, I've lived in worse places.'

Reba turned up her nose again. 'It's difficult to imagine anything worse than this!' she exclaimed disdainfully, although in truth, she could imagine it, with a lot of work, looking quite beautiful. Perfect for lovers sharing a meal as the sun set in a blaze of glory. The flight of fancy shocked her back into the present, and she cleared her throat hastily. 'No sane woman would ever consider living here with you!'

His answer was as finely honed as a lancet. 'She would if she loved me.'

The fatal cut devastated her, and her response was pure reflex. 'You'll never get me beggaring myself for love!' she retorted, then, when the hidden import struck her, she turned a shocked gaze on Hunter. She found his eyes had hardened dramatically. He looked as if he had a bad taste in his mouth.

'No, but you've no qualms at all about prostituting yourself for money, have you, Reba?' he charged witheringly.

Colour stormed back into her cheeks. 'I'm not doing that!' she protested faintly.

'No?' Hunter taunted as he settled himself comfortably against the porch rail. 'Your heart isn't on offer, so that only leaves your body. You're giving that in return for Eliot's wealth. Perhaps you can think of another name for it, but I sure as hell can't.'

His words scarred her mind, leaving her adrift in the sea of his contempt. That was exactly what she was doing. Coldly, calculatingly. Yet he couldn't know it was from necessity, never from greed. Even if she attempted to tell him, what good would it do? It wouldn't miraculously make him love her again—or stop her marrying Eliot. She had given him her word, and he didn't deserve to be hurt.

It came as quite a shock to feel Hunter trail the backs of his fingers down her left arm. She jerked, feeling scalded, and almost spilled the hot coffee down herself.

'You have soft skin, but a heart like a steel trap,' he declared insolently, once again using that proprietorial tone which said he had the right to touch her any time he liked. Instantly she made to move away, but his fingers had gone lower and captured her hand. He raised it so that her engagement-ring caught the light.

'That's some rock you're wearing. You must have done something really spectacular to earn it!'

Reba caught her breath at the insult. 'I could kill you for that, Hunter! You know damn well it's my engagement-ring!' she said shortly, and this time managed to pull herself free, mainly because he didn't try to stop her.

Hunter grinned, but he looked more like a wolf baring its fangs. 'Don't put yourself down, tiger-eyes, I know just how...spectacular you can be,' he rejoined mockingly.

The studied cruelty very nearly shattered her beyond all hope of recovery. It was the knowledge that he wanted to see her fall apart which gave her the necessary grit to stand and fight. It wasn't easy, but it was absolutely essential.

'Mmm, I never thought of it quite like that, but you know, you're right. It's a beautiful ring,' she agreed, holding it up to let the facets flash blindingly as she blinked back tears.

Hunter's eyes narrowed as the grin disappeared, and she had the doubtful satisfaction of knowing she had scored a hit. 'Big isn't beautiful; it's just flashy.'

Not for the world would she tell him she agreed! She clicked her tongue. 'You're only saying that because it's Eliot's ring and not yours,' she sniped scornfully.

Crossing his arms, and thereby drawing attention to the magnificent planes of his chest, Hunter shook his head. 'I'd never give my woman a ring like that. She wouldn't need it to know she belonged to me.'

'No, you'd just put a ring through her nose!' she sneered.

Hunter shook his head again. 'I'd give her love. That's more important than a piece of jewellery. All that ring says is, Look how much money I've got!'

Reba's eyes became feline slits as she set down her half-empty cup on the rail beside him. Her anger was pure fabrication. 'From your point of view, maybe. From mine it tells me Eliot loves me!'

Hunter stood abruptly as rage suddenly glittered from his eyes. 'Do you measure his love by the gifts he gives you? Just how would you rate these ear-rings?' he asked, taking her lobe between his fingers to remind her of the diamond studs she wore.

His touch stung, like his scorn, and instinctively she pulled away. 'Don't touch me!'

The contempt in his smile hurt her. 'Hands off unless I pay for it, tiger-eyes? Eliot doesn't know what a prize he's getting. Oh, you'll be a loyal little wife, so long as the gifts keep coming, won't you?' Swift as a jungle cat, Hunter pounced, catching her by the shoulders, fingers digging into her skin until she winced. 'You don't know what love is. All you know is this...'

Reba tried to fight him, bracing her hands against his chest in a desperate attempt to keep him at bay, but he was far too strong for her. With shaming ease he closed the gap and she just had time to witness the glitter in his eyes before his head swooped, cutting off light and escape. His mouth came down hard on hers, taking possession of her lips with a mastery she had never forgotten. But where there had once been tenderness, now there was only steely purpose. Knowing her pleasure-points, he used her weakness against her, teeth nipping and tongue stroking at the sensitive skin, making her shiver at the exquisite sensation.

Curling her hands into fists at his shoulders, she willed herself not to respond, to resist his attempt to part her lips, because she knew she would surely be lost if he did. But she wasn't proof against the feel of his hard male body pressed so tightly against her own softness. It started up an ache in the pit of her stomach. An anguished sob caught in her throat. She knew him so well. The feel and taste of him were like a part of her, and she longed to give in to that insistent throbbing.

As if he guessed it, Hunter's hands left her shoulders, tracing a pathway of heat down the silken skin of her back. Shivering, she barely felt him tug the halter-top free of her shorts until his hand found and claimed her breast. She gasped in delight, and with a growl of triumph he let his tongue find the goal it sought, thrusting into her mouth, beginning a caress so erotic that she was lost. Her tongue flickered to join his, engaging in a duel of mounting passion as she began to move her body against his in a message as old as time.

When he released her mouth, her head fell back helplessly, allowing him to plunder the silken arch of her throat, while his fingers pushed aside the cotton of her top to seek the swell of her breast and tease her nipple into an aching point. Instinctively she arched into that touch, and her fists relaxed, fingers delighting to the feel of his skin, clinging on as his head descended to take the place of his hands.

The touch of his mouth on her breast made her cry out, a strangled sound which turned to a whimper of pleasure as the rough stroke of his tongue sent a shaft of sensation through her. Shuddering in his arms, she was his to command, so it was all the more shocking to find herself suddenly thrust away. She was left to stand swaying before him, lips bruised from the touch of his, eyes dazed from the emotions which had assailed her.

His breathing scarcely altered, Hunter raked her up and down with his eyes. 'Whatever you're getting from my cousin, it doesn't come close to satisfying that sexy body of yours.'

Shamed colour stormed into her cheeks as she realised how comprehensive his victory had been. 'Damn you!' she muttered thickly, pulling the cloth over her breast with fingers that trembled. When she looked up again, her eyes were defiant. 'You're wrong. I get all the passion I need from Eliot!'

'You're lying, tiger-eyes. You're forgetting I saw the hunger in you last night. You're going to find money is a poor substitute for passion, Reba.'

Her heart kicked in her chest as she remembered that Hunter didn't know she still loved him. And although it hurt her to know that he could see her love as mere lust, it was her salvation. He could think what he liked, so long as he never guessed the truth. For, if he did know, he would have the ultimate weapon.

'Perhaps, but I'm going to marry him all the same.'

Hunter pushed himself upright and took the one step which brought him before her. 'If you imagine for one moment that I'm really going to let you marry my cousin, you're mistaken,' he pointed out coldly, and at last the gloves came off.

The declaration took the air from her lungs. 'What do you mean?'

His smile had all the charm of a hungry tiger. 'What do you think I mean? Whatever our personal feelings, Eliot is my cousin. He's family. If you think I'll calmly sit back and watch you destroy him, you don't know me very well.'

She was beginning to think he was right. He had the means to ruin all her plans, and she didn't know how to fight him. She swallowed hard. 'What are you going to do?'

'Exactly what you think I'm going to do,' he gibed.

If it were just for herself, she wouldn't even be bothering, but her mother was involved, and she had to try everything. 'Isn't there . . .? Isn't there some way we can reach an agreement?' she asked huskily, licking painfully dry lips.

PLAY "LUCKY HEARTS" AND YOU GET . . .

★ Exciting Harlequin Presents® novels — FREE

★ Plus a Lovely Simulated Pearl Drop Necklace — FREE

THEN CONTINUE YOUR LUCKY STREAK WITH A SWEETHEART OF A DEAL

1. Play Lucky Hearts as instructed on the opposite page.

2. Send back this card and you'll receive brand-new Harlequin Presents® novels. These books have a cover price of $3.25 each, but they are yours to keep absolutely free.

3. There's no catch. You're under no obligation to buy anything. We charge nothing — ZERO — for your first shipment. And you don't have to make any minimum number of purchases — not even one!

4. The fact is thousands of readers enjoy receiving books by mail from the Harlequin Reader Service. They like the convenience of home delivery. . .they like getting the best new novels months before they're available in stores. . .and they love our discount prices!

5. We hope that after receiving your free books you'll want to remain a subscriber. But the choice is yours — to continue or cancel, anytime at all! So why not take us up on our invitation, with no risk of any kind. You'll be glad you did!

NOT ACTUAL SIZE

*This lovely necklace will add glamour to your most elegant outfit! Its cobra-link chain is a generous 18" long, and its lustrous simulated cultured pearl is mounted in an attractive pendant! Best of all, it's **absolutely free**, just for accepting our no-risk offer!*

HARLEQUIN'S
LUCKY HEARTS

With a coin — scratch off the silver card and check below to see what we have for you.

106 CIH AW69 (U-H-P-01/96)

YES! I have scratched off the silver card. Please send me the free books and gift for which I qualify. I understand that I am under no obligation to purchase any books, as explained on the back and on the opposite page.

NAME

ADDRESS   APT.

CITY   STATE   ZIP

Twenty-one gets you 4 free books, and a free simulated pearl drop necklace

Twenty gets you 4 free books

Nineteen gets you 3 free books

Eighteen gets you 2 free books

All orders subject to approval. Offer limited to one per household and not valid to current Harlequin Presents® subscribers.

© 1991 HARLEQUIN ENTERPRISES LIMITED.   **PRINTED IN U.S.A.**

Disdain etched itself on to his handsome face. 'Bribery, Reba? Are you offering me sexual favours for my silence? You really must be desperate!'

Reba had never felt so humiliated, and if she weren't as desperate as he joked, she wouldn't have put herself in such a hopeless position. 'Damn you, Hunter!' she cried in a tight voice, and pushed past him to the steps. As she reached the bottom, his voice halted her for a second. She looked up to find him leaning against the post, watching her through narrowed eyes.

'Did I tell you what a pleasure it was to see you again, tiger-eyes?'

She wanted to scream. To kick and scratch and bite. 'No, and I don't believe you!'

A small smile curved his lips and he leant forward over the bar. 'You never used to have such a temper, Reba. Could it be frustration?'

She wouldn't dignify that with an answer. With a smothered cry she turned and fled, tearing up the track as if the devil were after her. Hunter watched her go, a grim smile playing about the corners of his mouth. Then he looked down at the object he held in his hand—a tiny diamond stud ear-ring. Tossing and catching it, he whistled a silent tune and wandered back into the house.

CHAPTER SIX

REBA was out of breath and distinctly dishevelled by the time she reached the house, and, with the memory of her encounter with Hunter still ringing in her head, wanted only to escape to her room where she could nurse her wounds. But, like the best-laid plans, hers were dashed when she heard her name being called just as she crossed the hall. Dearly though she would have loved to ignore the summons, she reluctantly altered direction and entered the lounge.

Four heads turned towards her, and each face registered a different reaction to her appearance. Eliot looked shocked, Eleanor startled, and Mrs Thorson merely raised an eyebrow, while the fourth member of the party seemed actually concerned.

'Good lord, Reba, whatever have you been doing? You look a mess!' Eliot declared in horror at the sight of her.

Her flight, and there could be no other word for it, had not been without mishap. She had even fallen once. A glance downwards showed that there was still dust on her clothes and, she suspected, on her face too. She certainly didn't look as if she had been having an idle stroll about the island, but before she could form any sort of explanation, she was forestalled.

'Oh, don't be so ridiculous, Eliot!' the newcomer reproved him in a voice at once soft and steely. 'It's obvious she's had a fall. Did you hurt yourself?'

Reba studied the beautiful young woman, who had to be the expected guest. She hadn't known what to expect, but one thing was certain: the concern was absolutely genuine. So, whatever the problem between this woman and Eliot, it wasn't caused by herself. Relieved, she pulled a wry face, patting at her shorts and releasing a tiny cloud of dust. 'Not really. I went for a walk, and I'm afraid I did trip over, but the only thing I hurt was my pride,' she explained, inviting the young woman to laugh with her, which she did with a light, tinkling sound.

'Oh, *pride*! I've had my share of bumps too. It's funny the way some people react to them, isn't it, Eliot?' she challenged him with a slyly mocking glance.

Over by the window, Eliot stiffened. 'Meaning what, precisely?' he demanded, his neck going pink, much to Reba's surprise.

His tormentor shrugged. 'Nothing, unless you can think of something.'

Seeing battle-lines about to be drawn up, Eleanor interposed herself hastily. 'You've been gone hours, Reba. We expected you back at lunchtime,' she remarked over-brightly.

Reba frowned, her own worries temporarily forgotten. Clearly something had happened in the past, and this was not the first exchange today. Considering that Eleanor, knowing that, had been the one to invite this other woman, it was strange that she should now be trying to defuse the situation.

'I'm sorry. I was under the impression that Eliot would be gone most of the day,' she apologised at once, wondering if she had misunderstood, and not liking to think the deception had been intentional. From Mrs Thorson she received an apologetic smile which she would have sworn was sincere.

'They returned much sooner than I expected, my dear. Usually Eliot would have remained for lunch before returning.'

'He was in a hurry to return to your side. Isn't that so, Eliot?' the newcomer added sweetly.

Eliot's jaw worked furiously. 'I'm warning you, Sib, shut up!'

The recipient of his threat merely laughed, although Reba noted there was something at the back of her eyes which she couldn't quite interpret. However, she said nothing more, and Reba was left wondering yet again what it was that this woman had done to antagonise the usually easygoing Eliot.

Mrs Thorson looked relieved. 'Do come and meet Sibyl, now that you're here.'

Sibyl Haggerty rose to greet Reba with a friendly smile. She was young, barely into her twenties, but she had that kind of loveliness which would blossom into real beauty as she matured. There was no mistaking the gentle kindness in her eyes, but she was no push-over, as her taunting of Eliot had shown. Reba was left with the distinct impression that there was more to the young woman than met the eye.

'Eliot was right, you are beautiful,' Sibyl declared with a friendly smile. At the same time she cast a sideways glance at him. 'I'm glad you held out for marriage.'

It was instinctive to look for Eliot's reaction, and Reba found she wasn't surprised to see that tide of red creeping further up his neck. What was going on?

'You've grown into a very lovely young woman, too, Sibyl,' Mrs Thorson declared fondly. 'Don't you think so, Eliot?'

'I didn't know she had it in her,' he responded crushingly, and Reba saw Sibyl's teeth snap together before she managed to laugh.

'The trouble with Eliot is that he will always see me as the silly schoolgirl who had a terrific crush on him!'

Sibyl teased, glancing back at Reba. 'He didn't like it when I grew up and stopped hero-worshipping him.'

So that was it? thought Reba. Sibyl had grown up and discovered other men, and Eliot had been piqued? It was a little childish, but many men hated to be reminded of their age. She hadn't expected that of Eliot, but then she really didn't know him all that well yet. However, she usually trusted her first instincts, and returned the young woman's smile, knowing it was impossible not to like her. 'I hear you've been in Europe,' she said politely.

Sibyl grinned. 'My mother thought it would be good for me, because the French have such style.'

'They're supposed to be perfect lovers, too, or aren't you going to kiss and tell, Sib?' Eliot exclaimed rather nastily, and all four women stared at him.

It was Sibyl who found her tongue first. 'I never kiss and tell, Eliot. If I started, I might not stop,' she said very softly, and Eliot took a swift breath.

'Reba, my dear, shall I order you a light lunch? You must be quite famished,' Mrs Thorson intervened hurriedly.

Reba shook her head, as much in confusion as negation. She really didn't understand what had brought on that unpleasant scene, and she hadn't expected Eliot to be so unchivalrous. 'Please don't bother. I'd rather just go and clean myself up. Eliot was right—I am a sight.'

'As you wish, dear, but I'll have coffee and sandwiches sent up all the same,' Mrs Thorson decided, and Reba didn't gainsay her, although her appetite had vanished a long time ago.

'I'll keep you company, Reba,' Sibyl proposed instantly. 'I have to collect something from my room.'

Although she recognised an excuse when she heard one, Reba didn't put her off. It might prove interesting to hear what she had to say. They crossed the hall in companionable silence, and it was only as they began mounting the stairs that Sibyl finally cleared her throat.

'I like your name. It's rather exotic, like you,' she declared a little nervously, as if that wasn't what she had intended to say at all, and Reba laughed, wondering where this was heading.

'Well, maybe I'm not as exotic as I seem. I can't help the way I look, you know. It's just genes.'

Now Sibyl placed a hand on her arm and brought them both to a halt. Her pretty face was serious. 'Have you known Eliot long?'

Reba frowned slightly. 'Several months. Why?'

The other woman seemed to be debating with herself what to say, then pressed on. 'This is more difficult than I thought. Oh, hell... I wanted to know if you love Eliot.'

Reba knew she could never have anticipated this, and hesitated a moment before she answered. 'I must do, if I'm going to marry him,' she proffered uneasily.

Sibyl uttered a faint, diffident laugh. 'I know, you think I'm either crazy or jealous, but...I like you, Reba. I just wanted to say, don't let Eliot's charm fool you. If you're sure you want to marry him, don't wear blinkers. I hope you'll be happy, I really do.' With that she turned and ran up the last remaining steps and disappeared down a corridor.

Reba frowned after her. This was all she needed! First Hunter had told her she would never marry Eliot, and now here was this young woman issuing a warning so veiled that she didn't know what it was. She carried on up to her room slowly. With her bedroom door safely shut behind her, Reba leant back against it and closed her eyes wearily. Everything was going wrong, just when it should have been going right. How foolish she had been to think Hunter would accept her presence even though he hated her. It hadn't occurred to her that he would try to stop the marriage. She didn't know exactly what he would do, but she couldn't allow it to happen. Her mother's operation had been given the go-ahead. It would only be a matter of weeks now. What on earth would she do if...?

Her eyes came open and she straightened abruptly. She didn't want to think about that now. Walking across to the dressing-table, she removed her ring and reached up for her ear-rings. She would shower and change, and when—— Her thoughts stopped there as she discovered the missing diamond stud.

She plopped down on the stool, her mind shooting back to that moment on the veranda when Hunter had clasped her ear-lobe. The stud must have come loose then, only she hadn't noticed it. She laughed, a raw sound. Was it any wonder, with everything else that was going on? Her neck ached as she rolled it to ease the tension.

Damn him for looking so good. Her physical attraction to him had been as instant and strong as on their first meeting. Everything within her responded to him—he was her mate. The other half of her which made her whole. No other man could do to her what he did. No other man had the power to turn her world upside-down.

Then she laughed again, with even less humour. Hunter might have a body which turned her mouth dry at the thought of touching it, but he despised her. Thank God he didn't believe she still loved him. At least one of the gods must have been on her side, because heaven knew, in those first moments she had done nothing to protect herself. It wasn't pleasant to know he thought of her as merely lusting after him, but after acting so foolishly she had to be grateful for small mercies.

Not that she was given long to be grateful, because at that precise moment a knock came on the door and, before she could respond to it, Eliot slipped inside and quickly shut the door. She resented the intrusion, but bit back her first angry words, remembering that he would soon have the right to do more than enter her room. The thought chilled her. She had only ever given one man that right, and it foolishly felt like betrayal to put Eliot in his place.

Consequently, her words were rather clipped. 'I was just about to take a shower, Eliot,' she informed him as she stood up.

The smile he sent her as he crossed the room was cajoling. 'I won't keep you. I only wanted to apologise for being so insensitive just now,' he soothed, and attempted to take her in his arms, a manoeuvre she sidestepped neatly. Misunderstanding her motives, he swapped cajolery for concern. 'Are you sure you didn't hurt yourself?'

'I'm perfectly all right. Nothing that a shower won't put right, anyway,' she reassured him, wishing he would just go, because she really didn't have the patience to deal with him right now.

Eliot missed the veiled hint. 'That's good, sweetheart. Er—you and Sibyl have a chat, did you?' he continued, seeming to find the contents of the dressing-table fascinating.

Reba watched him picking things up one by one, and began to feel uneasy. 'Briefly,' she admitted, staring at his averted head in mounting concern.

Eliot dropped a pot of cold cream and slipped his hands into his trouser pockets. 'What did she have to say?' he enquired idly, wandering to the window.

Reba knew the question was anything but idle, and her heart lurched. What was wrong? She swallowed to moisten a dry mouth. 'Just girl-talk. What did you think she said?' she challenged softly, eyeing his suddenly tense back.

Eliot turned with a laugh. 'Oh, nothing. But Sib can sometimes exaggerate. It isn't always wise to believe everything she says.'

'I'll keep that in mind,' she acknowledged levelly, and once again saw colour rise up his neck.

As if realising he might have made a tactical error, Eliot dragged a hand through his hair. 'She should never have been invited here,' he snapped irritably. 'She never would have been if I had been consulted!'

Reba didn't doubt it for a second. The question was, why? 'Well, she's Eleanor's friend, so I doubt you'll have to see much of her.'

With a deep sigh he came and put his arms round her. 'You're right, darling. Sensible Reba. No wonder I love you so much,' he groaned, kissing her with a mounting passion. Even so, it didn't arouse her as Hunter's kiss had, and she had to fight the memory to return the embrace. Fortunately Eliot didn't appear to notice, and smiled at her when he finally released her.

'You're wonderful. I'd better let you get on and take your shower,' he declared, but paused as he reached the door. 'Oh, by the way, you didn't run into anybody in your travels, did you?'

She was glad he was too far away to see her cheeks turn pink, or they would have revealed her lie as she shook her head. 'No. Just a lot of butterflies and birds.'

Eliot nodded. 'Good. I'll see you in a little while, then,' he promised, and finally left.

Reba stared blankly at the door. Sibyl had hinted, and Eliot had questioned, but about what? Just what had happened between them to cause all this alarm? And alarm was what she was feeling. Trouble was coming at her from all sides, and she felt less and less able to cope with it. Tiredly she combed her fingers through her hair, wishing she could ease the tension inside her. She had come here with such high hopes, full of determination to make Eliot a good wife. She had always known how hard it was going to be. She couldn't love him as she did Hunter, but he was deserving of love, and she was going to give him all that she had left. She would make it enough, so that he would never regret asking her to marry him. She had vowed to construct a life for them that would leave no place for regrets, and any she did have would be firmly locked away. She would make herself be happy, content to make Eliot happy too. She was paying a high price, but it would be worth it.

If only she didn't feel as if she was sitting on a time-bomb. Any minute it would go off, but she didn't have a clue as to who would be left standing when the smoke finally cleared.

It was hot. It was also very late. Reba hadn't even bothered to attempt to go to bed. It was too hot to sleep. She had come upstairs a long time ago, after the strangest evening. It had been almost surreal, as if, by common consent, they were all playing their own version of charades. Eliot had stayed by her side, but it hadn't escaped her that he had watched every movement Sibyl made. Conversation over dinner had been stilted, with nobody doing justice to the food, and it had been a relief when, much later, Eleanor had decided to put on some music. Eliot had immediately asked Sibyl to dance but, after a vigorous exchange of words, he had left her in order to partner Reba, remaining with her until, having had enough, she had invented a headache and escaped to her room.

As she stepped from beneath a cool shower, drying herself and slipping on a delicate confection of silk with strategic lace inserts, Reba had nothing to cheer about. She had Hunter's threat hovering over her head, and a fiancé who was turning into a stranger before her very eyes. On top of that, she could feel the beginnings of a very real headache. Towelling her hair, she shook it out and left it in a dark halo, knowing the heat would dry it in no time. Switching off the light, she stepped back into the softly lit bedroom and came to an abrupt halt.

From his comfortable position stretched out on her bed, Hunter let his eyes rove over her, and there was nothing Reba could do to stop her body responding to that blatantly sensual examination. Nor would she raise her arms in an instinctively feminine gesture of protection, even though her nipples had hardened immediately, and now thrust proudly against the inadequate lace covering of her nightdress. She had run once today; she wouldn't run again, even if there had been somewhere to run to.

'Very nice,' he murmured huskily, and the fine hairs on her skin shivered to attention.

Damn him! 'What are you doing here, Hunter?' she demanded, very much aware that her voice sounded far too croaky for comfort. He was still in those disreputable jeans, though this time the sleeveless T-shirt was black, and he had trainers on his feet.

He grinned, taking devilish pleasure from her reaction. 'Right now, enjoying the view. You always were damn good to look at, Reba, although touching you had a definite edge, remember?'

How to forget? The memory of his touch was an invisible brand, marking her always as his. She could guess why he was here, and her thumbs began to prick ominously. 'You know, all I have to do is scream, and the family will come running. What do you think they'll do when they find you here?'

To her annoyance, Hunter laughed. 'Well, tiger-eyes, if you're looking for Eliot to defend your honour, you're going to be mightily disappointed. Besides, we both know you aren't going to scream,' he added, his voice dropping to a level which strummed at her nerves, undermining them.

He was so sure of her that it stung her into action for her pride's sake. Her response was to send him a flashing glance of dislike. 'Oh, do we?' she taunted, and had opened her mouth to defy him when he raised his hand and something caught the light, making her pause.

Slowly Hunter sat up. 'Carry on, I won't stop you. We'll see what dear Cousin El and Aunt Helena have to say when I explain I came to return this,' he said, holding between thumb and finger what she now easily recognised as her missing ear-ring. 'Naturally they'll want to know how I came by it. Of course, if you've already confessed to visiting me, you've nothing to worry about, have you?' His eyes held hers, challenging her to deny his unspoken claim that she had said nothing.

She stared him out as long as she could, but it was only a matter of time before her eyes dropped, and she clasped her hands across her waist. 'Damn you!'

'So, why don't you come over here and make yourself comfortable while we talk?' He patted the bed invitingly.

Reba's nerves fairly leapt out of her body. Join him on the bed? He had to be kidding! That would be taking recklessness to the point of self-destruction. 'If you've come to return my ear-ring, just leave it and go. We have nothing else to talk about.'

His brows rose at that, infinitely mocking. 'You're forgetting the little matter of your marriage to Eliot.'

'No, I'm not,' she denied, taking a step closer to emphasise her point. 'I've had time to think, too. You aren't going to say anything, because, whether I'm a gold-digger or not, Eliot will never believe a word *you* say!' she countered triumphantly.

'Are you really prepared to take that chance?' Hunter challenged quietly, and somehow it was all the more powerful for that softness.

Reba's heart lurched. She had missed something. Something vital. She knew it as certainly as she also knew that she didn't know what it was. Yet she could not back down. 'I know Eliot!' she claimed, conveniently forgetting the doubts of the evening.

Hunter rose from the bed with a cat-like movement, prowling towards her with such deliberation that she had to use all her control not to back away from him. 'Good,' he accepted, as he halted no more than a hair's breadth away from her. 'Then you'll know exactly how he'll react when I tell him something entirely different. You see, I intend to confess to him that you and I were lovers. And he'll believe me, tiger-eyes, because I'll tell him about this,' he declared, and his hand came out to brush across her stomach before coming to rest at the top of her left thigh. 'A very interesting place to have a mole.'

Reba gasped and flinched away. 'You wouldn't!' she protested faintly, hurting in a way she had never thought possible at the idea he could do such a thing.

He watched her unwaveringly until she was ready to scream, then he smiled, teeth flashing whitely in the darkened room. 'No, you're right, I won't. You see, tiger-eyes, I'm not going to tell Eliot anything. You are.'

She knew she had paled, and icy fingers clutched her heart. 'What?'

His amusement vanished. 'It's quite simple. You tell him your way, or I'll tell him mine. You can save face by telling him you've changed your mind, but if you leave it up to me, I'll tell him about us.'

Meaning she was damned if she didn't, and damned if she did. Whatever she did, she lost. 'You can't be serious! That's no choice at all!'

Hunter's face hardened, closing up, making it impossible to read his expression. 'Take it or leave it, that's up to you, but make up your mind to this. You aren't going to marry Eliot.'

She couldn't believe that in a few short weeks they had come to this. 'How could I ever have loved you?' She didn't realise she had spoken the words aloud until Hunter answered them in a voice of honed steel.

'You never loved me, Reba, you just loved what you thought I had. I didn't find being taken for a ride, however inventive you were, very edifying. You should never have played around with me, tiger-eyes, and you should never have come this close to me again. Everything has to be paid for, one way or another,' he told her coldly, and she felt the ice of it chill her blood.

'You're determined to get your pound of flesh, aren't you?' she said flatly, seeing her family's happiness vanishing before her eyes, destroyed by the man who had meant the whole world to her. There couldn't be a more savage wound.

Hunter laughed, and it was the most cynical sound she had ever heard. 'Chin up, sweetheart, there is a plus side.'

She looked at him in disbelief, and saw in his eyes a look which made her heart miss a beat. 'Wh-what do you mean?'

'I'll take you instead.'

There were a few awful seconds after he had made that bald statement when her heart thudded wildly inside her chest, and she thought she was about to faint, but that release was not allowed her. She stayed conscious, her shocked gaze interlocked with his.

'What did you say?' The query was automatic, to give her time to recover. She didn't doubt what she had heard, and he knew it well enough.

Even so, he obliged her by repeating it for devilish reasons of his own. Hunter's blue eyes glittered. 'I said, I'll take you. You weren't the only one to hunger last night, tiger-eyes. You're a hard act to follow. Nobody quite measures up to your passion, and they never will until I've sated myself with you. I want you in my bed again, and I'm prepared to pay for the privilege. Not marriage, but I can give you all the money your avaricious soul requires.'

Was there no end to the hurt he could inflict? With a sound of disgust, she stepped away from him. 'You can't seriously think I would agree to become your mistress!' Her voice broke on the dreadful word, and she swallowed back a wave of sickness.

'Those are my offers, take them or leave them,' he told her bluntly.

Ice began to settle about her heart, freezing it off. 'You never used to be so cruel!'

His lips curled sardonically. 'I hadn't had the pleasure of knowing you then. They say a good woman can do wonders for a man, but it's nothing to what a bad one can do.'

Reba caught her breath. 'I'm not bad!' she protested in a choked voice, and he grinned.

'No, in certain areas you're very good. That's why I don't understand this hesitation on your part. You always used to enjoy making love with me,' he taunted, closing the gap between them once more and raising her chin with a forceful finger.

Her eyes flashed him a look of withering contempt. 'This wouldn't be love, only sex!'

Hunter was unscathed; his gaze slipped away from hers and followed the glide of his finger along her jaw and down her throat. It stopped where his finger rested over the frantically beating pulse, and his mouth took on a sensual curve. 'Call it what you like, the end result will be the same.' His eyes lifted to hers again. 'Or have you forgotten? Perhaps I should give you a timely reminder,' he said silkily, and his hand moulded her throat, turning her head to meet the descent of his.

She only had time to mutter a strangled, 'No!' before his mouth cut her off and she was plunged pell-mell into a dizzying world of the senses. Her hands came up at once, but the instant they found his chest they turned traitor, fingers spreading out to encompass more of him instead of pushing him away.

He was so clever. He didn't use force—he didn't need to. He only had to touch her and she went up in flames. He was an addiction from which she could never break free. No other man could raise her temperature so that it shot off the scale with only the caress of his lips and tongue. Within seconds she was a trembling mass of ultra-sensitive nerves, craving his touch on every part of her. While his tongue continued its erotic dance with hers, her breasts surged into painful arousal, longing for the touch of his hand, so that in the next instant her hand moved to clutch his wrist, tugging until he finally obeyed and allowed her to pull his hand down and settle it firmly on her breast.

With a moan of pleasure she felt his fingers close around her turgid flesh, moulding it, teasing it, rubbing his thumb across the aching point until she arched into his touch, shivering at the dark delight. At the same moment his mouth left hers, allowing him to gaze down into her glazed eyes. Finger and thumb found her nipple and squeezed gently. She gasped.

'Is that what you want, tiger-eyes, or this?' he growled, and his head lowered, mouth enclosing her, suckling avidly at her proud flesh and sending a shaft of pleasure down through her.

Reba moaned again, helplessly, fighting an inner battle which pitted the knowledge that she shouldn't be allowing this to happen against her body, which recognised only that she wanted him badly. And there in the background was a small voice saying, You can have him. You can have him again, if only you agree to his offer. A tear struggled to the corner of her eye, for she knew that knowledge debased her feelings for him. It should be love, not sex!

. That gave her just enough strength to pull away from him and take a few trembling steps to freedom. 'Leave me alone!'

He followed her. 'You don't mean that.'

'Yes, I do!' Angrily she turned away, making a futile bid for escape which he subdued by pulling her back against him, his arms holding hers pinned to her sides.

'No, you don't,' Hunter laughed huskily in her ear. 'Your body tells the truth your lips would deny. I only have to touch you like this...' One hand glided up to her breast, brushing aside the silk to cup her in his palm and tantalise her with a slow circling movement. Her head fell back against his shoulder as she caught her breath. 'And you're mine,' he declared, his lips caressing her neck at every word.

Reba closed her eyes, unable to deny it. He knew her so well; there was no place for her to hide. 'Let me go, Hunter,' she whispered brokenly, acknowledging defeat.

'You still haven't given me a yes or no.'

He was pushing her too far! His words were destroying something he didn't believe existed, and which she would not lay open to his scorn again. A large lump of emotion rose to block her throat, and she answered with difficulty, 'It's yes to letting me go, and no to your rotten deal!'

From the way he went still, he hadn't been expecting that. The next moment she was released, and turned to face him. His expression was shuttered once more. 'Publish and be damned, Reba?'

With trembling fingers she straightened her nightdress. 'However much I hurt you, I don't deserve to be treated like this,' she returned, with all the dignity she could muster.

One mobile eyebrow lifted as he stepped away from her. 'Hurt me? Hell, I guess you could say my pride was hurt. I'm not used to being rejected. I don't think any man is. When you hit a man where he lives, tiger-eyes, you can't expect to get away with it.'

'Considering how you think of me, I would have thought you'd think you had a lucky escape,' she countered bitterly.

'From the clutches of your sticky little fingers, I did. Which leaves my wanting of you unfettered by romantic complications. We still want each other, Reba, and it's as strong now as it ever was. So don't kid yourself you'll find it hard going to bed with me.'

That was a calculated slap in the face, telling her in no uncertain terms that the violent attraction she felt was too powerful to fight. There would have been nothing shameful in the knowledge if she had been free to choose with her heart, or if he still loved her, but neither of those things applied. She couldn't deny she wanted him, but she loved him too, though God knew why, when he could make the suggestion he had. Yet the heart obeyed only its own rules, otherwise she would hate him, as her brain said she must.

She looked at him, unaware of the sadness in her eyes which made his own narrow. 'You've changed.'

'You should be proud of your work, Reba. Now there's one less gullible male around.'

Only a cynical one in his place. She wasn't proud of that. 'I think you'd better go.'

Hunter's teeth flashed as he grinned wolfishly. 'Oh, I'm going, but I'll be back. Sleep on what I said. I'll give you thirty-six hours to give me your answer—after that I go straight to Eliot.'

Reba didn't have a reply. All she could do was watch him disappear out on to the balcony without a backward glance. Damn him, he had her trapped and she knew it. She could twist and turn, but the result would always be the same. Eliot was lost to her. She knew how he felt about his cousin; he would never stomach the knowledge that she and Hunter had once been lovers. All she could do was save face by breaking off the engagement herself.

But what about her mother's operation? Perhaps Eliot would still loan her the money? He knew how desperately she needed it. Why, he had even told her she *should* have come to him. Surely he would accept a business arrangement? It was a slim hope—the only one she had. She didn't dare think about what she would do if he refused.

Whatever happened, she would never agree to become Hunter's mistress! It wasn't even an option, despite the fact that he had offered her the money he thought she wanted. Well, she might need it, but nothing would induce her to accept his terms. Because he was only offering her sex, and sex was no substitute for love. Foolish or not, love was what she wanted from him, and nothing less.

Oh, it would be so easy to give in to the lure of passion, to tell herself it didn't matter that she was virtually confirming the lie she had told him, and was bartering herself for money. But it did matter, because saying was one thing, doing another. Give in, and he would have no cause to doubt.

No, she would not be accepting his offer, however tempting the siren call was to her battered heart, because she was so terribly afraid that if she did it would devalue her love for him, and the memory of that was all she had to cling on to.

CHAPTER SEVEN

'I KNOW, why don't we send a message down to Jacob to make the yacht ready? We're sure to be much cooler out on the water,' Eleanor declared over breakfast the following morning when, despite the early hour, the island's atmosphere was already beginning to resemble a hothouse.

'That's a marvellous idea, Nell. You'll come too, won't you, Reba?' Sibyl responded immediately, and Reba had to admit that a day's sailing would be perfect. She needed to get away from the island, and all chance of running into Hunter. He had given her thirty-six hours, and she intended to use all of them. Who knew? She might even think of a way of beating him.

'I'd love to,' she accepted without hesitation.

'How about you, Eliot?' Eleanor turned to her brother.

'Oh, Eliot isn't a very good sailor. He won't mind staying behind,' Sibyl answered for him, and Reba's heart sank as she knew she should really stay behind with him.

However, Eliot, who had been listlessly picking at his food, looked up quickly. His smile was tight. 'If Reba wants to go sailing, then I'm going with her,' he declared, reaching for Reba's hand and enclosing it in his own.

Sibyl tossed her head and laughed. 'Isn't it amazing what love can do? He'd never brave seasickness for me.'

No, thought Reba, wondering why he was doing it now. An ugly suspicion grew inside her that his joining the expedition wasn't for her benefit, because he knew

117

she loved sailing, but because he didn't want to let Sibyl out of his sight. She didn't like thinking that way. It seemed disloyal, which was ridiculous in the circumstances, but she couldn't help it. He wasn't responsible for the mess she found herself in and, until she broke the engagement, he was her fiancé and deserved her loyalty.

Unaware of her thoughts, Eliot responded by getting to his feet. 'Maybe I don't want to stay here and stifle either. I'll have a word with Neville,' he finished, and disappeared indoors in search of the butler.

'Shall you be coming with us, Aunt Helena?' Sibyl asked into the hiatus which accompanied his departure. The mood over breakfast had been peculiarly tense, with everyone making too much effort to appear normal.

'No, dear. You young ones couldn't really relax with me there. I shall be quite happy here while you four go and have a good time. I'll have a picnic made up for you, then you can make a day of it.'

That was the cue for them all to leave the table, and they made their way back up to their rooms to get ready.

It didn't take long for Reba to slip a bikini on beneath her shorts and top, and collect into a bag anything else she thought she might need. She was just leaving her room to go back down to the hall when she heard a sharp cry, followed by the sound of someone falling. Hurrying to the top of the stairs, she was in time to see Eleanor at the bottom, trying to push herself to her feet.

'Here, let me help you,' she called, running down and giving the other woman a helping hand. 'Have you hurt yourself?' she asked in concern.

'It's my ankle. It turned under me. I only fell three steps,' she explained, wincing at a brief attempt to put weight on the injured leg.

Reba helped her to the nearest seat and knelt down to examine the ankle. It was swelling already. 'It looks like a bad sprain, I'm afraid.'

'Oh, damn. That means no sailing for me today.'

Sibyl had joined them by now, and heard her friend's disappointment. 'We won't go. There will be other days for sailing. You agree with me, don't you, Reba?'

Before she could answer, Eleanor interrupted. 'Don't be silly, you must go. There's no point in us all sitting around just because I was idiot enough to sprain my ankle. I'll curl up with a book, and you can tell me all about it afterwards.'

She wouldn't be budged, and in the end they gave in. They made her as comfortable as possible before Eliot drove them down to the harbour. Despite the bad start, Reba felt excitement grip her, as it always did at the thought of being out on the water, hearing the rush of waves beneath the hull and bringing the sail up into the wind to get maximum speed.

It was a while since she had been on a boat—not since... Hastily she brought the curtain down on the memory. That had been the last time she had seen Hunter until just two days ago. She shivered, not wanting to think about Hunter and the ultimatum he had issued. He wouldn't be with them. For a whole day he would be left behind, and she could relax.

'You girls go on ahead. I'll bring the hamper,' Eliot suggested, once they had stopped, which was how he came to be some way behind them when they walked down the jetty to where the yacht lay moored.

There was one man aboard her, and the size and shape of him caused Reba's steps to slow. It couldn't be! But it was. At that moment Hunter looked up from his task to wave. She couldn't see the smile on his face, but she guessed at the mockery. She would have given anything to turn back then, but with Eliot behind her she had to go on. At her side, Sibyl uttered a soft cry of delight and hurried forward.

'Hunter! What in the world are you doing here?'

In one lithe movement, Hunter jumped down on to the jetty and swung her round in a laughing embrace which threatened to tumble them into the water. It shouldn't have surprised Reba to realise they knew each other, for they moved in the same circles. All the same, it was a shock. By the time Sibyl was on her feet again, there was the faint hint of colour in her cheeks. A shaft of undiluted jealousy ripped through Reba as she looked on, closely followed by despair. They looked at ease together, happy—everything her relationship with Hunter no longer was.

It was a moment before she realised that she was no longer alone. Eliot arrived in time to witness the greeting. His reaction took her by surprise.

'What the hell is going on? Let go of her, Hunter! You can't seem to keep your hands off anything that doesn't belong to you!'

Sibyl looked to be about to send back a pithy retort, but Hunter squeezed her arm bracingly before he let her go, and took a step forward, arms akimbo. 'You can only be engaged to one woman at a time, cousin, and, as far as I'm aware, that woman's Reba,' he pointed out sardonically, gaze drifting to where Reba stood in a state of near-paralysis. His eyes silently queried whether his statement was still correct, and glittered mockingly when she tipped her chin.

Anger and anxiety made an uncomfortable mix inside her. What was he doing here? He had said she had thirty-six hours to think over what he proposed, but his words had been as much a warning to her as a taunt to Eliot.

He wasn't going to allow her to forget he had the whip-hand, and time was passing.

Eliot seethed angrily. 'Sibyl is a guest here, and under my protection!'

Hunter looked him up and down. 'Yeah, and I know how protective you can be!'

Drawn from her own disturbed thoughts by the exchange, Reba saw Eliot turn white. When he spoke, anger had turned to bluster. 'What are you doing here, Hunter? And what the hell were you doing on my boat?'

As if he had got the response he expected, Hunter smiled. 'Making ready to sail. You ordered the yacht out, or have you changed your mind?' he drawled.

Eliot coloured angrily. 'Where's Jacob?'

'Jacob's hurt his hand, and the last thing he needs is to get the wound infected. As I was here, and I'd nothing planned for the day, I offered to take his place. So, are you going to keep wasting time or are you coming aboard?'

Sibyl glanced round the frozen tableau, then reached out to take Hunter's proffered hand. 'We're coming aboard, of course,' she agreed, and within seconds was on deck.

Reba stared at Hunter in impotent fury. He hadn't had to offer at all, but she just knew he couldn't resist it. Damn him!

'Well?'

She looked at Eliot, expecting him to refuse, willing him to, but once again he surprised her. 'Take this and get out of the way,' he said ungraciously.

Hunter, barefoot and bare-chested, and clad in cut-off denims, took the hamper Eliot thrust at him and jumped aboard effortlessly. His blue eyes drifted to Reba who was still standing on the jetty. 'Coming?'

He knew as well as she did that she couldn't be the only one to refuse to go. She was trapped and they both knew it. Stepping forward, she held up her hand, and as she did so her eyes sent him a withering look.

'If we drown, I'll sue you,' she managed to joke, although as far as she was concerned the day was irretrievably ruined. All she could do now was grin and bear it.

The satisfaction on his handsome face told her he knew exactly how she was feeling, and with something approaching a flounce she turned away and took a seat as far away from him as possible. She need not have bothered, for Hunter forgot about her in an instant as he prepared to cast off. She couldn't help watching him then as he moved about, and perversely it did her heart good to see his lithe grace as he manoeuvred the beautiful craft away from the jetty and headed her out to sea. He had strength when it was needed, and subtlety too, and he used both when controlling a boat or making love to a woman.

She wished she could hate him for what he was doing, or at the very least not love him, but that was impossible. Her heart wouldn't be dictated to, even in her own defence.

'Do you know Hunter?' Sibyl asked from beside her, and she started out of her reverie, colour washing into her cheeks as she wondered what she might inadvertently have revealed.

'Hunter?' she parroted, trying to get her brain to work, knowing she must sound like a fool.

'Hmm. You were watching him with the strangest expression—I thought perhaps you knew him,' Sibyl expanded, making Reba feel worse.

She managed to shrug. 'I met him the other night. It wasn't exactly a pleasure,' she admitted, almost smiling at the irony.

Sibyl looked amused. 'He probably made a pass, just to get at Eliot.'

Reba gave a half-hearted laugh. 'Hunter seems very protective of you,' she remarked, recalling that brief interchange a moment ago.

The other woman's face took on a tender expression. 'I've know him since I was little. Hunter's a great guy, the sort you can take your troubles to. Which is more than can be said for some.' Her gaze moved to where Eliot was just disappearing below, and there was no mistaking her meaning.

Reba felt as if she was the only one in the dark. Even Hunter seemed to know what was going on, and it was clear whose side he took. 'Why don't you like Eliot?'

Sibyl tensed, and the smile she gave was stiff. 'Surely it doesn't matter why I don't like him, so long as you do,' she responded.

Once Reba would have thought so, but not now. 'Why didn't Eliot want Hunter to touch you?'

Sibyl gathered up her bag and gave her a bland smile. 'You'll have to ask him that. I'm going down to the cabin to change. Are you coming?'

The subject was closed, but it left Reba unsatisfied. However, right now she had her own problems to think about. 'I'll be down in a minute,' she promised and, when she was sure the other woman was out of sight, she crossed to where Hunter stood at the wheel.

He cast her glance as hot as the sun which beat down on them. 'Alone at last!'

She was as angered by his quip as by the fact that every nerve she possessed responded to a glance which had been deliberately provocative. 'What on earth do you think you're playing at? You gave me thirty-six hours, remember?' she gritted through her teeth, eyes blazing with fury.

Undaunted, his lips curved into a sensual smile. 'Just keeping an eye on my investment, tiger-eyes.'

The look curled her toes and nudged her into instant denial. 'I'm not your investment!'

'Yet,' he reminded her, and laughed huskily when she paled. 'You'd better go and see to your fiancé. He was looking decidedly green just now,' he prompted, and turned his attention back to the task in hand.

Reba was left staring at his back and shoulders, already gleaming with effort and exuding a tantalising scent which brought back poignant memories and turned her knees to jelly. Time seemed to stand still as she fought an almost overwhelming urge to run her hands over his tanned flesh, to use her tongue to savour the essence of him. The sheer eroticism of it scorched her, but not nearly as much as the flame which burnt in his eyes as he turned and caught her unguarded expression.

'The sex was always good, wasn't it, tiger-eyes?' he taunted softly.

His choice of words brought her to her senses, and with a strangled groan she turned to gather up her bag and stumble below. It was sex now, not making love, and it was a barometer of how his emotions had changed.

She met Sibyl on her way up. Now wearing a dashing yellow bikini beneath a flimsy beach-top, she looked fresh and appealing.

'Are you all right?' Sibyl asked anxiously as Reba almost missed a step.

'I'm fine, I just haven't got my sea-legs back yet,' she lied, and took a steadying breath. 'Have you seen Eliot?'

'He's in the master cabin, dying. He said he doesn't want to be resurrected until we land somewhere. I don't know why he bothered to come.'

Sibyl's scorn made Reba glance at her sharply. Her next words were a shot in the dark. 'I imagine he wanted to stop you telling me something he wants kept secret,' she said evenly.

'He should know me better than that!' Sibyl retorted, then caught her breath as she realised what she had said.

'So there is something,' Reba pounced. 'Are you in love with Eliot?'

Sibyl laughed, and the tone of it would have been denial enough. 'I had a crush on him once,' she admitted calmly, 'but that passed. If you want to know what we fell out about, I'm afraid you're going to have to ask him. He might tell you the truth—or he might not. It all depends on how he thinks you'll react. Eliot likes to manipulate people.'

Reba frowned. 'In what way?'

The other girl sighed heavily. 'Oh, hell, haven't you learnt yet that Eliot always likes to get his own way?' she demanded, before nimbly climbing the ladder on to the deck.

Reba stared after her, more confused than ever. She couldn't match up Sibyl's description of Eliot with her own. He had never tried to her to do anything she didn't want to do. He was kind and generous, not deserving the kind of hurt Hunter was forcing her to give him. But she wasn't going to think about that today. Hunter could wait for his victory.

She carried on to the main cabin, but there was no answer to her soft knock, so she left Eliot alone and retreated to the nearest cabin. Stripping off her clothes, she revealed the skimpy black bikini she had chosen to wear. She wished now that she had chosen something

which covered more of her, but she hadn't known then
that Hunter would be on board. Sighing, she found her
tube of sunscreen and went to join the others.

Sibyl was talking with Hunter, laughing as he gave her
a lesson in steering. Reba grimaced at the anger the sight
produced, and deliberately turned her back. Coating
herself with sunscreen, she spread a towel out and lay
down, doing her best to ignore what was going on,
although her ears seemed to pick up the slightest sound.
Every laugh sent knives into her flesh, and irritably she
turned over, exposing her unprotected back to the sun,
but too dismayed by her own jealousy to care. Burying
her head in her arms, she tried to block the sounds out.

'You'll burn. I'll put some cream on you,' Hunter declared drily from somewhere above her, and she looked
up.

That wasn't what she had in mind at all, and she shook
her head. 'I'll be fine. You're steering the boat,' she refused. Having him touch her would be the closest thing
to torture she could imagine.

Predictably, he didn't listen. 'Sibyl's doing OK on her
own.' Squatting down beside her, he picked up the tube
of cream, holding her wary gaze with his own mocking
one. 'You're not scared, are you, Reba?'

It was just spur enough to make her lie down again.
When he chuckled, her hands balled into fists, and she
waited in a state of acute tension for the first touch of
his hand. She was right, it was torture—but of the very
sweetest kind. He made no pretence of doing a simple
task, as she had known he wouldn't. He used the cream
to relearn the soft curves of her body, unfastening the
catch of her top to allow himself free rein down to the
minuscule briefs.

Reba bit back a moan with her teeth clamped to her
lip, but it was virtually impossible to stop herself from

moving beneath his expert touch. She gasped when his long fingers brushed the sides of her breasts, and jerked as if she had been stung when he began the same ministering technique on her legs. Yet, in a moment of lucidity, she knew his hands were clinging to her, as if he couldn't bring himself to let her go, and her heightened senses caught the laboured sound of his breathing. He was not immune, responding to the way he was making her respond. They had always been explosive together, and nothing had changed.

Then it was over, his hands were gone, and her aching, aroused body felt bereft. Sanity said she should be glad, but it was hard to be sane when he was so unbearably close to her.

'Don't stay out too long,' Hunter warned gruffly, and the tension in his voice was the only thing which made her look up. She could only see the back of him, but the rigidity was telling. Then he turned, eyes burning hot, the evidence of his own arousal there for her to see. Reba gasped, feeling her stomach clench. He saw, and there was an ironic curve to his mouth as he turned away.

Reba buried her head in her arms and willed her body to stop trembling, and her heart to cease its wild pounding. He had done it on purpose. It didn't matter that he had been aroused too. He had wanted to underline his claim, and had done so. She had even forgotten that they were not alone. Anyone could have seen, and though they hadn't been making love, there had been very little room for doubt that that was where they had been headed.

How long she lay like that she didn't know, but when she finally stirred it was to discover that Eliot had decided to brave it topside. Hunter was at the wheel again, while Sibyl sat beside him. Scrambling to her feet, Reba went to join Eliot, giving him a sympathetic look.

'Hi, you're looking better,' she greeted. 'Where are we headed?'

'For one of those islands,' Eliot returned, pointing ahead to where a group of three or four was slowly getting nearer. Sure enough, a quarter of an hour later, the yacht sat at anchor in the sheltered bay of a tropical island paradise. They ferried the picnic things ashore and set them up in the shade of some palms.

Eliot, restored by the return to land, shed his shirt and slipped on sunglasses. 'OK, Hunter, that's everything. You can return for us in an hour or so,' he pronounced offensively.

Sibyl gasped, and Reba automatically held her breath, knowing the statement would not go down well. From where she stood, she saw Hunter's eyes narrow dangerously, and waited for fireworks.

'I'm not your servant, cousin. I was doing you a favour. As far as I'm aware, you don't own this beach, and I have a perfect right to sit on it. Of course, it's your privilege to try throwing me off it.'

It was Sibyl who stepped into the breach. 'Stop being such a boor, Eliot. There's plenty of food and drink, and at least he's earned his share of it.'

'Has he earned his share of you, too?' Eliot asked nastily, making Reba gasp in distaste at his indelicacy. Hunter wasn't pleased either, and he growled as he stepped forward.

'Take that back, cousin, before I ram my fist down your miserable throat!' he threatened.

Eliot backed off hastily, not doubting that Hunter was fully capable of carrying out his threat. 'All right, all right, I apologise!' he said quickly, carefully staying out of reach.

Hunter's teeth flashed as he smiled contemptuously at his cousin. 'Very wise. Now I'm going for a swim—anyone care to join me?'

Reba didn't so much want to go with him, as to wash away the taint of that unpleasant scene. Ignoring the others, she ran swiftly down the golden sand, diving into the first convenient wave.

When she surfaced some time later, it was to discover a fair head bobbing along beside her. 'Eliot shouldn't have said that,' she said, and Hunter laughed wryly.

'Eliot shouldn't say or do a lot of things.'

Sweeping her hair back from her face, Reba frowned. 'I'm glad you came to Sibyl's defence,' she said stiltedly, and his smile widened.

'There's no need for you to be jealous, tiger-eyes. I've always looked on her as a sister. You're in a different league. A woman like you can give a man sleepless nights,' he drawled silkily, and even in the beautifully cool water she felt her blood heat. 'But there's an age-old cure for them which we'd both enjoy. As soon as you make your decision.'

'You're so sure I will agree to anything you say, aren't you?' she snapped, kicking herself away from him.

'Aren't you?' he taunted.

'There are times when I really hate you, Hunter Jamieson!' she cried, and swam away, heading for the shore as fast as she could go.

Unfortunately, Hunter kept pace with her easily. 'It's the other times I'm interested in.'

'The other times I just despise you!' she gibed, and spurred herself on to greater efforts, all to no avail because he passed her easily and was waiting on the beach when she finally waded ashore. She slapped away the hand which he held out to her and jogged up to where Eliot sat.

'The water's lovely, you should have come in,' she told him, accepting the towel he held out to her and rubbing vigorously at her hair.

'You didn't seem to miss my company,' he sneered, nodding to where Hunter had joined Sibyl and now sat propped against a palm a short way away.

It was on the tip of her tongue to tell him to stop being so childish, but she was glad she had resisted when she found Hunter was watching them. On impulse she put her hand on Eliot's thigh, and could almost feel Hunter's eyes narrow. 'Of course I missed you, darling,' she cajoled, leaning across to kiss him. His response took her by surprise. She had been expecting a brief caress, but Eliot jerked her into his arms, swinging her down so that he rested over her, and kissed her with a depth which should have stirred her, but instead left her chilled.

He didn't seem to notice. When he lifted his head to look down at her, his eyes glittered with satisfaction. 'That should show them!' he muttered thickly. 'But just for good measure...' His head lowered and he kissed her again, but this time Reba felt her gorge rise at being so used, and she gathered all her energy to push him away.

'Stop it! I won't be used to score points, Eliot!' she warned, letting him see how angry she was.

At once he became apologetic. 'Sorry, darling, but those two made me so mad! Forgive me?' he wheedled cajolingly, and she stared at him coldly. He seemed to think he only had to apologise and everything was all right again.

'No, I don't think I will,' she stated flatly, and the look of surprise he gave her might have made her laugh had she not seen the anger which followed it.

'What do you mean?' he demanded through clenched teeth, and she smiled thinly.

'I mean, if I didn't know better, I'd say you were jealous that Sibyl seems to prefer Hunter to you!' she accused.

Eliot stared at her as if he couldn't believe what he had heard, then, with a face like thunder, he scrambled to his feet. 'You'll regret that!' he snapped, before spinning on his heel and striding away.

Reba didn't watch him go. As she rested her head on her arms she was aware of a sense of relief. There was a side of Eliot she hadn't seen before, and she didn't like it. He had had no right to try and use her that way.

'Lunch is ready,' Sibyl called out, but Reba had lost her appetite.

She pretended to be asleep, and the combined effect of virtually sleepless nights plus the warmth and peace soon turned pretence into reality. When she awoke some time later, everything was so quiet that she thought she was alone, but when she lifted her head and looked around her, she discovered Hunter still apparently asleep beneath the palm-tree. It was Eliot and Sibyl who were missing, and a quick scan of the tiny bay showed no sign of them. She frowned, and jumped when Hunter spoke.

'Sibyl swam back to the boat some time ago, and Eliot still hasn't returned.'

'What?' The word jerked out of her, because his eyes were still shut. The lids lifted indolently then, and she was speared on the end of his blue gaze.

'You heard.'

'Eliot hasn't come back? How long has he been gone?' she queried, concerned because she had been responsible for his going off, and anything could have happened to him.

'A couple of hours. Don't worry, he's probably just sulking somewhere. What did you say to him, anyway?'

She scowled at his amusement. 'None of your business.'

Hunter moved, making himself comfortable on his elbow, the better to watch her. 'I can probably guess,' he said with a grin, and allowed his gaze to rove over her. 'This is like old times. I've always enjoyed watching you sleep.'

Reba caught her breath, remembering times when the intensity of his gaze had managed to draw her from sleep. 'I wish you'd stop saying things like that!'

He sighed and, much to her dismay, rose nimbly to his feet, only to drop down beside her, so close that their breath mingled. 'What would you have me say?'

She sat up at once, hugging her arms around her legs. 'Nothing. I'd rather you said nothing!' she claimed through a tight throat.

'Liar!' he countered, and in the next instant his hands came out and grasped her shoulders, pulling her backwards until she overbalanced and tumbled flailing on to the sand. Before she could rally, his thigh came over hers, pinning her down, and he loomed over her, balancing on his elbow. The other hand framed her chin, forcing her gaze to meet his.

'Do you love him, Reba? Is it going to break your heart to let him go?' he taunted mockingly.

Hurt spiralled inside her, because that was what she had felt when she had had to spurn him. 'You bastard!'

His jaw tensed and his eyes flashed warningly. 'I am what you made me, sweets, and whatever that is, you want it.' His hand gentled, releasing her to run a tantalising finger across her lips. 'Has it been a long hard winter without me?'

Her eyes closed in pain. It had been endless winter. 'Don't flatter yourself!'

His voice dropped an octave. 'I wouldn't, if I thought you were going to fight me. Are you, Reba?' he whispered.

She opened her eyes at that, and stared at him, trying to probe beneath the surface. Once she had seemed to see so much in his eyes, but now there was only the reflection of herself. 'I should.'

'But you aren't?'

Her hands came up, touching the skin of his back and sending a frisson of pleasure skittering through her system. Everything seemed so simple in his arms. If she stayed there, nothing could hurt her. 'Dear God, I wish I knew how to!' she groaned, uncaring of what she might give away.

Hunter went perfectly still as triumph gleamed from his eyes. 'Capitulation, Reba?'

She didn't altogether know what it was, she only knew she was where she ought to be, and she was too weak to fight him. 'Damn you, Hunter!' she cursed thickly, and his eyes darkened a moment before his head lowered.

She received his kiss with a sigh of satisfaction, opening her lips to welcome him in, joining with him in a sensual exploration which rapidly descended into a battle. Neither could seem to get enough of the other, either with lips or hands. She didn't know when her top disappeared, only gloried in the wonderful feel of his powerful chest pressed to hers as he came down over her. Her back arched as he slid down her, open mouth finding the frantic pulse in her throat before travelling on to claim the aching peaks of her breasts.

Reba moaned, her nails digging into Hunter's shoulders as he laved her breasts with lips and tongue, her growing excitement bringing a groan to his own lips as she writhed beneath him. Needs held too long in check broke the bounds placed upon them, and they both plunged wilfully into the stormy seas of unleashed passion. She ached, so ready for him that she thought she would die if he didn't soon take her, and the thrust of his arousal was proof enough of just how much he wanted her.

Then, as if someone had turned on a jet of cold water, they both heard a cough. It shocked them into stillness, only the sound of their pounding hearts and laboured breathing echoing around them. Hunter raised his head, staring into her agonised eyes with a look of anger, frustration, and something more which was instantly hidden.

'Eliot always did have a rotten sense of timing,' he growled, then, pushing himself to his feet, he sent her one last scalding look before running down the sand and diving into the crystal waters. By the time Eliot erupted on to the beach, Hunter was yards from shore and Reba had struggled into her top, flinging herself down on to her front and burying her face in her arms to pretend to sleep.

Nothing was further from reality. Sleep had never been further off, and neither had peace of mind. These last few minutes had told her, even if she had been inclined to doubt it, that she could give in to Hunter's threat and share with him the rainbow hues of passion for as long as it lasted. But what might satisfy her body would leave her heart a desert, and she didn't think she could survive without love for long.

Only Eliot could save her, and he was no longer quite the man she had thought he was. Would he help her? She had to believe it, for if he didn't, what hope was there for her?

CHAPTER EIGHT

IT WAS still quite early. Reba stood at the water's edge, wishing the gentle crashing of the waves were as cooling as it sounded. Having tossed and turned and paced away the hours, she had finally decided enough was enough, and dressed and come down to the beach. Shading her eyes, she squinted off into the distance, noting the expanding banks of clouds to the east. It had to be the storm Hunter had foretold, and she wished it upon them. Anything to break the oppressive heat. She would have sworn that it was getting worse by the hour, and the only cool things about her were her feet as she stood in the shallows.

Sighing, she slowly paddled on with listless steps. It was hardly surprising that she had barely slept. It was decision time. After those moments on the beach, she had expected Hunter to visit her last night. When he hadn't, she had not known whether she was glad or sorry. If he had come, would she have allowed him to make love to her? Allowed? The ache of frustration which had stayed with her told her she would have been an equal participant.

Well, he hadn't come, and so she had not given him her decision. She wasn't even sure what she was going to say. No, that wasn't true. She knew what she might have to say, but she still clung to one slim hope. If only Eliot would come through for her, then she need not suffer the further heartache of a loveless relationship with Hunter.

Stubbing her toe brought her painfully back to the present, and she looked up. There were rocks running down to the water in several places, virtually dividing the beach into a series of private little coves, and she was just debating whether to wade round into the next one or turn back when the sound of voices reached her, stopping her in her tracks. She recognised them easily and, because they belonged to Eliot and Sibyl, she didn't retreat tactfully, but took a few cautious steps closer instead.

'Oh, it's you. What do you want, Eliot?' Sibyl greeted him with every sign of distaste.

Eliot's laugh was equally unfriendly. 'Just a private chat.'

'As far as I'm concerned, we have nothing to say to each other,' Sibyl retorted frigidly.

'I want to know why you're here,' Eliot demanded angrily, and it was almost possible to see Sibyl smile.

'I realised what happened wasn't my fault, and I decided I was no longer going to take the blame. I despise you, Eliot, and I came here to let you know how much. Eleanor is my friend, and I'm not going to allow you to destroy that friendship.'

'That's your only reason?'

'What other reason could I have?'

'If you have any plans to tell Reba about us, forget them, otherwise I'll make sure you're very sorry,' Eliot threatened.

Sibyl's laugh revealed that she was not alarmed by his aggressive noises. 'I'm already sorry I ever met you. Listen, you—you toad, I may have had a blind crush on you once, but you cured me of it when I discovered you were cheating behind my back even as you tried to put your ring on my finger!'

Sand ground underfoot as Eliot moved. 'I ended the affair months ago, just as I told you I would,' he retorted through gritted teeth.

'And as I told you, you don't know how to be faithful to one woman! It wouldn't be long before you were up to your old tricks again!' Sibyl shot back contemptuously. 'My God, you even tried to deny it until I told you I'd seen you with my own eyes!'

'You never would have found out if Hunter hadn't told you!'

'And I'm eternally grateful that he did. If Hunter hadn't told me about your on-going affair with that waitress, I might have ended up marrying you!'

Dear God, so that was what it was all about, Reba thought distastefully. Eliot and Sibyl had been virtually engaged, but he had also had a mistress. When Sibyl had found out, the engagement had been broken. It shocked Reba to realise how little she knew about the man she had been going to marry. She had never considered he could be unfaithful, but any doubts were ruled out by Eliot's next reply.

'You know, you're even more attractive now you've grown up and learnt to fight back. If I had you now, then I doubt I'd want to stray. We're both adults, and you wanted me once. I still want you, Sib,' he pronounced, and Reba could hardly believe her ears.

Neither could Sibyl, and when she spoke it was with loathing. 'You're sick! You're supposed to be engaged to Reba!'

'What she doesn't know won't hurt her. If we're discreet, I can have you both.'

Reba didn't wait around to hear the rest of Eliot's cajoling words, or Sibyl's reply. She had heard quite enough already, and was battling a violent need to commit murder as she back-tracked up the beach.

Finding her sandals where she had left them, she made her way up through the trees to the house. On the terrace, the table was set for breakfast, but remained unoccupied. It made her feel faintly hysterical, for everything looked normal, and yet she had just discovered that the man she was engaged to was a stranger to her.

How could he seem one thing and yet be another? She had believed she owed him her commitment, but now she knew she owed him nothing. If she hadn't been able to give him love, she had thought she could respect him, but who could respect a man who didn't know the meaning of the word fidelity, and who thought nothing of taking a mistress even before he was married? Not that she believed for one minute that Sibyl would agree. They had both had their blinkers violently removed.

'Good morning, my dear,' Mrs Thorson greeted her gently, and Reba swung round in surprise, so lost in her thoughts that she hadn't heard the other woman arrive.

'Good morning.' The words came out stiffly as she did her best to act as if nothing out of the ordinary had happened. It didn't fool the older woman.

'Are you all right, Reba? You look very pale.'

Glancing down at her engagement-ring, Reba angrily twisted it round and round her finger. Suddenly it seemed important that someone spoke honestly. 'I'm fine... Well, not really. I know I'm doing this in the wrong order, but you're here, and... You see, I've just decided I can't marry Eliot after all.' She raised her head and met the other woman's unflinching gaze. 'You don't seem surprised.'

Mrs Thorson sighed rather wearily. 'I'm not, although I am disappointed. I believe you would have made him a good wife, and he really needs that. I suppose you can't tell me why...?'

Reba bit her lip. Eliot would come unstuck one day, when his mother found out his true nature, but the revelation wouldn't come from her. 'It's personal,' she said, with a shake of her head.

Helena Thorson winced. 'I'm not blind, my dear. I know my son has faults. I was hoping you could change that, but if he isn't the man for you, then you shouldn't marry him. Never marry a man for the wrong reasons, Reba. I married for security and status. I love my children, although I never loved their father. That's why this family and its position is so important to me. It's all I have.'

So many things were becoming clear this morning. 'And it's why you resent Hunter, because he took away part of your son's inheritance?'

The older woman sent her a look of grudging respect. 'You have a quick mind. Yes, that's why I resent him. He inherited land which I had always looked upon as Eliot's.'

Reba frowned. 'Yet he doesn't seem to resent you.'

'Why should he? He now owns more valuable real estate which he doesn't need. He'll never use it, and neither will he sell it to us!' Mrs Thorson argued frostily. 'I'm afraid, my dear, that if you're trying to make me see Hunter in a different light, you're wasting your time. You really haven't known him long enough to know him at all well.'

On the contrary, Reba knew him a great deal better than this woman ever would. She also knew that Helena Thorson would never change her mind. He had stolen from her son, and that would forever condemn him. She didn't like the injustice, but she had more pressing problems right now.

'May I use your telephone?'

'Of course you can, dear. And if I see Eliot, I'll tell him you want to see him.'

Reba stiffened. He was the last person she wanted to see, but it had to be done. 'If you wouldn't mind. Thank you for being so understanding. I know this is a difficult situation.'

'I'm sure I'll survive it.' A sudden gust of wind caused Helena to look seawards. 'The storm will be here shortly. Hunter was right about that. Nothing will be putting out to sea now.'

Squinting up at the advancing clouds, Reba knew she was right. Somehow it fitted in with her mood. Sunshine and peace would have been totally out of place. Excusing herself, she went to the telephone. She had an important call to make, and what she did next hinged on the answer. The time difference was a problem, but she couldn't afford to wait another few hours. Somewhere in England, the telephone rang.

'Hello?' A sleepy voice answered, one which she recognised from countless consultations.

'It's Reba Wyeth, Doctor. I'm sorry to ring so early, but something has come up, and I need to know exactly what's happening about the operation,' she apologised, twisting the cord around her fingers nervously.

There followed sounds of someone pulling himself together in a hurry. 'Oh, yes, Reba. I was going to get in touch. Everything is going to plan. The flight is booked, and the hospital expects your mother in ten days. All you have to do now is get the money to them by the end of this week at the latest. Can you do that?'

Reba closed her eyes. It was the best of news, and the worst. She rallied swiftly. 'Of course. The money will be there, and so will I, to meet the plane. Thank you for all your help, Doctor.'

'My pleasure, Reba. Goodnight.'

'Goodnight,' she returned, and set the phone down. Well, that was that. She definitely had to have the money. There were still two options, and she chose the one which would bring her the least grief.

Pushing herself to her feet, she went in search of Eliot.

She found him in his bedroom, and wished for a better setting. This wasn't going to be easy, and a bedroom didn't seem to be the right place for what she had to say. The door was open, and she could see him out on the balcony, but she knocked anyway. He was clearly surprised to see her in the doorway, but from the way he smiled she knew he didn't suspect that his early-morning conversation had been overhead.

'I'm sorry, darling, have you been looking for me? I was about to come and ask you if you wanted to go snorkeling,' Eliot exclaimed cheerfully, advancing on her with his arms held out.

Reba, having taken a few steps into the room, held up her hand to stop him. If he touched her, she might just hit him. 'Actually, I was looking for you to return this.' She held out the ring which she had removed from her finger. 'I can't marry you, Eliot.'

He was stunned, staring at the ring as if it were dangerous. However, that didn't last long, and within seconds his expression was one of anger. 'What do you mean, you can't marry me?' he demanded furiously, then sudden inspiration twisted his handsome features. 'It's Sibyl, isn't it? She's got to you, damn her!'

The violence of his response made her flinch, but she stood her ground. 'Sibyl has nothing to do with it. The truth is, I thought I could marry you, but I can't, because I don't love you. I thought I could grow to love you, but I know I can't.' It wasn't all she wanted to say, but she still had a favour to ask him, and however much against the grain it went, she couldn't afford to burn her boats. So she said nothing of what she had overheard.

Ignoring the hand which held the ring, Eliot closed the gap and took her by the shoulders. 'But I love you, damn it!'

If he loved her, then his idea of love was a world away from hers. It didn't matter anyway, and Hunter's ultimatum had no bearing on this. After what she had learned, she couldn't have married Eliot, even for her mother's sake. 'I'm sorry.'

Eliot thrust her away, snatching the ring from her and tossing it across the room. 'Sorry? What the hell good is sorry?'

Reba chewed on her lip, knowing she was reaching the crux. 'Better sorry now than later,' she added, silently acknowledging the truth of that in the light of current events.

'Spare me the platitudes!' he snarled, the charming veneer shattered, and turned away abruptly. 'If you've said all you came to say, you might as well go.'

Reba hesitated a moment before pressing on. 'Actually, there is something I wanted to ask you.'

He twisted round and stared at her for a long while, before starting to laugh. 'You know, I was quite forgetting your mother. I had an ace up my sleeve, and I didn't know it!'

Reba felt the first stirring of unease. 'What do you mean?'

Eliot's smile broadened as he quickly recovered his poise. 'I mean, you still need the money, don't you, sweetheart?'

The meaningless endearment chilled her. 'You know I do. You said you'd help,' she reminded him staunchly.

'Of course I did,' he agreed expansively, laughing again. 'I wanted you. I'd have agreed to anything to get you. Did you honestly think I'd just give you the money without getting something in return?'

Her head went back, as she realised the depth of his deception. 'You lied.'

'Not necessarily. After all, I still want you, and you still need the money. You can have it, providing you marry me.'

Reba shook her head slowly, wondering how she could have been so deceived. 'Sibyl was right, you are sick!' she flung back at him, uncaring now of what she revealed.

That shook him, and he stiffened. 'She did tell you!'

Now it was her turn to smile. 'No, I overheard. You weren't as careful as you thought you were! Well, you're wrong about me, Eliot. I might need the money, but I won't give in to blackmail. So you can take your offer and...' She didn't finish the sentence, knowing he would get the message. Spinning round, she left the room, slamming his bedroom door behind her as she went.

Seeking the sanctuary of her room, she pulled a chair out on to the balcony and collapsed into it. He was hateful, and she knew she was well out of it, but that didn't help her. Her options had dwindled rapidly, so that there was only one left. Hunter. He no longer had the power to destroy her relationship with Eliot, but he had made her an offer she was now forced to consider. He wanted her, and had said he would pay for the privilege. At least it would be a bargain, not blackmail. If only she didn't love him so, it would be easier to live with his hate. Yet wasn't it poetic that, having destroyed their heaven, she should share his hell?

A stray gust of wind blew her hair into her face, and she looked up in surprise, realising that the wind had got up, and the clouds which had threatened on the horizon not long ago were now a great deal closer, and very much darker. Reba had never witnessed a tropical storm, but she had seen plenty of pictures of hurricanes and the damage they could cause. It made her sit up and wonder just what they could expect. She had never liked thunder and lightning, and this promised to give her both, in spades.

By the time she went downstairs again for lunch, the wind was much stronger and the advance guard of clouds was already chasing across the sun. She wasn't surprised to find everyone on the terrace, all edgily watching the sky. Eleanor hobbled to her side with the aid of a stick, her ankle still securely bound.

'I was just about to come and get you,' she said, grimacing as she shifted her weight and sent pain up her leg.

Reba quickly pulled a chair across and helped her to sit down. 'Really?'

Eleanor smiled her thanks. 'Yes. The storm's going to be bad, and I didn't know if you were prepared for it.'

'I'm not. I hate storms,' Reba admitted, shuddering. She vaguely wondered if they should be doing something. Surely in all the films she'd ever seen storms were the sign for frantic activity?

Sibyl said as much when she came to join them. 'Eliot should do something!' she declared, then frowned as her eyes followed the hand Reba used to push the hair from her face. 'You're not wearing your ring.'

Reba pulled a wry face, studying her ringless hand. 'No. Eliot and I have decided not to get married after all,' she said shortly, glancing over to where he stood beside his mother's chair. At the same moment he chose to look her way, and the expression in his eyes was chilling. She shivered, then shivered again as the sun disappeared behind a cloud, plunging them into sudden gloom.

Everyone looked up automatically, so they weren't aware of the grim figure who rounded the corner of the terrace until he spoke in a voice which dripped acid.

'I might have known I'd find you all out here playing happy families, instead of doing the sensible thing!' Hunter exclaimed in disgust. 'Hell, you haven't even had the sense to put the shutters up.' Having elicited their complete attention, he stood regarding them scornfully, hands hooked into the belt of his jeans.

'Really, Hunter, you go too far!' Mrs Thorson complained, only to be totally ignored.

'I told you several days ago the storm was coming. You had plenty of time to act. This storm isn't going to wait for you, you know. It's going to hit very soon and, believe me, it's going to hit hard!'

Eliot rounded on him angrily. 'There's plenty of time. The servants know exactly what to do.'

Hunter's lip curled nastily. 'Sure they do, and they're doing it. I sent them off to look after their own families before I came to see how you were doing.'

His aunt's jaw dropped at his effrontery, and it was the first time Reba had ever seen her really put out. 'You had no right to do that!'

'I agree. It's something you should have done yourselves, instead of standing around admiring the view.'

Stung by his tone, his aunt quickly rallied. 'For your information, we were doing no such thing. In fact, Eliot was just deciding what we should do,' she snapped, coming to the defence of her son.

Reba could have told her that Hunter would be manifestly unimpressed by that, and sure enough he came back with a blistering retort. 'Bully for him! Unfortunately the time for thinking was over a long time ago. Right now I reckon we've got an hour and a half, two at the most, to get this place protected before all hell breaks loose. Aunt Helena, you and Eleanor had better go inside and start closing all the windows. Eliot can help me with the shutters. I hope to hell the store's not locked, or we're going to be in real trouble.'

For once nobody seemed to challenge his right to give orders. He had transmitted his urgency to them, and without a word his aunt and cousin disappeared indoors.

'What can we do?' Sibyl asked, her serious face showing she had been through this before.

Hunter glanced around. 'There's too much loose furniture and stuff about for my liking. You'd better get as much of it put away as you can. You know the drill.'

'What about me?' Reba put in as the other girl hurried off.

'You come with me. Your job will be to fasten the shutters when we put them up. Think you can manage it without breaking a nail?' Hunter drawled sardonically, and it would have given her a great deal of satisfaction to hit him.

'Don't worry about me. I'm no shrinking violet,' she sniped, following as he and Eliot headed for the storeroom. Then her anxiety got the better of her, and she asked, 'Is it going to be bad?'

Hunter took his time to study the horizon. 'Well, we could be lucky and just catch the edge of it, but I wouldn't bank on it. The safest thing is to plan for the worst and hope for a miracle. Afraid, tiger-eyes?' he added, and the words were soft, not a taunt at all.

Her heart flipped over, but she swiftly shook her head. Not for the world would she admit she was terrified of thunder. 'Not if you're not,' she boasted, and something flickered briefly in his eyes.

His grin was lop-sided. 'You choose the damnedest moments, Reba! Come on, let's get moving. I don't much fancy getting caught in the open when the rain starts.'

They worked like a team, and it *was* hard work, for the shutters were by no means light. Reba followed behind, steadying and securing, while overhead the storm clouds built up and the wind brought white tips to the waves in the bay and the palms began to sway. From time to time she caught sight of the others, all now hurrying against time as thunder rumbled ominously in the distance.

The first drops of rain fell just as they were putting up the last few shutters, and within minutes the heavens had opened the floodgates. Their clothes were plastered to them when they finally dashed for the safety of the front hall, slamming the door behind them.

'You OK?' Hunter asked her as he watched her wipe moisture from her face, and she grinned.

'Just a little damp. It's quite refreshing, actually.'

He slicked back his hair with a laugh. 'You wouldn't think so in half an hour. If you were out in it then, you'd think it was trying to hammer you into the ground. But you'll be safe enough in here,' Hunter reassured her, flexing tired shoulders.

He had worked like a demon, helping a family whose ingratitude was highlighted by the fact that Eliot hadn't offered a word of thanks. She couldn't let it go by, though.

'Thanks for your help. We couldn't have done it without you, could we, Eliot?' she prompted, eyes flashing an angry message to her ex-fiancé.

It was not appreciated. 'Don't let us keep you. I'm sure you want to get back to your hovel.'

Reba couldn't believe what she was hearing. Rage bubbled like a cauldron inside her. 'If anything happens to him, Eliot, because you've sent him back out in this, I'll make sure you regret it! It's not only ungrateful, it's downright wicked!'

Before Eliot could respond to her scorn, Hunter stepped in. 'It's OK, I had no intention of staying here anyway. You'll be fine. Don't go out unless you have to. I'll be seeing you.'

Reba found herself staring at the front door which had closed behind his departing figure. 'How could you just let him walk away like that?' she demanded furiously.

Eliot shrugged. 'He's not my responsibility.'

Outraged, she stared at him in disbelief. 'Neither were you his, but he came to help you anyway. How could you send him away? Anything could happen to him out there!'

A short silence followed, and Eliot's face took on a sneer. 'It seems to me you're altogether too concerned about a worthless relative of mine. What goes on, Reba?'

Instantly her lids lowered, shielding her expression. 'Nothing goes on, except natural concern for another human being. You shouldn't have done it, no matter what your feelings are.'

He didn't like her reproof, and his mouth thinned. 'Well, I'm damn sure I'm not going out there to call him back now! Neither are you!' he declared, catching her by the arm when she took a step towards the door. 'You heard the man yourself. He said he wouldn't have stayed anyway.'

She shook off his hand, while admitting it was true. Hunter wouldn't have stayed where he knew he wasn't wanted, and it was only her natural fear for his safety which had made her so ready to go after him. Thinking logically, she recognised that the storm was still in its infancy, giving him plenty of time to reach his house before the worst hit them. Hunter knew what he was doing. He would be safe enough.

However, as the eerie darkness of the storm deepened into the darkness of night, the worst that she could imagine paled beside what was actually happening. The continuous noise of wind and rain, which grew in intensity as the hours went by, was punctuated by rolls of thunder and creaks and groans of tortured trees. But it wasn't until Reba heard objects flying about, crashing into whatever stood in their way, that worry turned to real fear.

Here they were, safe in their brick house, but the only thing protecting Hunter from the force of the elements was a rickety wooden structure which had barely taken her weight, let alone the pounding it must be receiving now. Unable to sit still, she had gone to her room, pacing up and down, her mind plagued with visions of his mangled body lying within the wreckage of his house.

She halted before the shuttered window. If anything happened to Hunter she wouldn't be able to bear it. The world was only livable-in for knowing he was in it somewhere, alive. In that instant she knew she had to go to him. Her dread of the thunder was nothing weighed against the awful possibilities. She had to know he was all right, or be there with him if something happened.

Hurrying back downstairs, she found a torch in the kitchen, and a raincoat in a closet in the hall. Then, before anyone could suspect what she was doing and attempt to stop her, she slipped quietly out of the front door.

The full force of the storm didn't strike her until she stepped away from the protection of the porch. Then the wind hit her like a truck and she barely kept on her feet. Bending double, she struggled towards the track, finding small relief once she was in its inadequate shelter. She was already drenched, the over-large raincoat clinging to her legs as she tried to hurry along in the meagre light thrown by the torch. Every time something crashed into the forest beside her she jumped, but when a palm crashed across the path ahead of her she screamed, the sound instantly taken away on the wind.

It was a nightmare journey, but she refused to turn back, scrambling over fallen trees, uncaring of the grazes her legs suffered. She only knew she had to get to Hunter. How long it took she never knew, but by the time she reached the sloping path down to his hut, she was exhausted. But at least, even to her inexperienced eye, the building looked intact. The only worrying thing was that there was no light breaking through the cracks in the shutters.

Her heart clenched. Where was he? Had he even made it back here? Biting down her fear, she fought her way up on to the veranda. When the door refused to open, she pounded on the wood with fists and torch.

Gasping for breath, she called out his name. 'Hunter! Damn you, Hunter, you've got to be all right! Hunter!' His name ended on a strangled cry as the door was pulled away from her and light spilled out, blinding her.

'What the hell——?' Hunter's voice was shocked into silence as he stared at her. 'I don't believe it! Get in here, you little fool!' he snapped angrily, grabbing a handful of sodden raincoat and pulling her inside, shutting the door on the unruly elements.

Reba took a staggering step before sinking tiredly to her knees. She felt quite light-headed, now that the constant battering of her body had stopped. Above her head, Hunter was muttering darkly.

'I thought I told you to stay indoors? What the hell did you think you were doing?' he demanded fiercely, squatting down beside her and tipping her head up rather ungently.

Reba blinked again as the light shone in her eyes. 'I know what you told me, but I was worried about you!' she snapped back, recovering some of her strength. 'Take that light away!' she grumbled, trying to push it away.

He resisted her by holding it beyond her reach. 'I'm trying to see if you're OK.'

'Of course I'm OK,' she scowled, then winced as her movement to brush her hair from her eyes brought a dart of pain. She took her hand down and stared at the blood on her fingers.

Hunter drew in a hissing breath. 'Sure you're OK. You're a mess, and you've probably got concussion, but Reba Wyeth is OK!' he rejoined sarcastically, rising and dragging her to her feet by dint of putting a hand under her arm.

Having come all this way, she didn't appreciate her reception. 'Stop shouting at me!' she ordered and, much to her surprise, burst into tears.

It must have surprised Hunter too, for he said nothing for a moment, then very gently steered her into the nearest seat. When next he spoke, his voice was gentler too. 'You're crazy, do you know that?'

Sniffing, she felt about her for a handkerchief, failed to find one, and wiped her eyes on her sleeve. 'Thanks a bunch!'

'For God's sake, Reba, you could have been killed, and for what?' he asked, easing her hair away from her face so that he could examine the wound.

'So could you, that's for what!'

Blue eyes, unbearably close, stared into gold. 'Such concern,' he taunted, but it wasn't a taunt, and her cheeks flushed.

She looked away, shrugging diffidently. 'Wasted on you, obviously. I should have known this ruin wouldn't dare fall down on the likes of you, Hunter Jamieson!'

'However it looks, structurally it's quite sound,' he informed her, and she jumped to her feet, her head narrowly missing his chin.

'Good, then I can go back again, now I know you're all right.'

Hunter was before her in a flash, barring her way. 'Not so fast. You're going nowhere.'

He could be the most insensitive brute! 'You can't stop me!' She squared up to him, and he laughed, albeit grimly.

'If you leave, then I'll only have to go after you, to make sure you are all right, which would then leave you worrying about me again. We'd end up doing this trip all night in the teeth of a storm. Maybe that appeals to you, but it doesn't appeal to me. So you're going to stay here, where I know you're safe, until the storm is finally over.'

'That could take hours!' she exclaimed, not really knowing why she was fighting, when leaving was the last thing she had thought of doing when she made her way here. But Hunter had a way of making her say and do things she'd never intended.

'I'm sure we can find something to do to while away the hours,' he mused suggestively. 'But first we've got to get you into some dry clothes and see to those cuts. Come along.'

Reba obediently rose to her feet. She knew she wasn't going anywhere, and wouldn't be even if there hadn't been a storm. Right or wrong, this was where she wanted to be. Her fear of the possibility of losing him had told her that. In the end, the decision had been taken out of her hands, and she would deal with the future when it happened.

CHAPTER NINE

HUNTER led the way into another room, which was as sparsely furnished as the first. By the lamplight she could see it was a bedroom, but there wasn't even a mattress on the bed. Surely, she thought, he didn't sleep on the floor? Yet before she could comment in any way, he propelled her to a corner of the room where a trap-door stood open, light gently flowing upwards from it.

'After you,' he urged politely, and because she instinctively knew he was expecting her to refuse, she carefully reached for the top step of the ladder with her foot, and climbed down. Hunter followed her much more agilely, closing the trap-door behind him, sealing them into the underground room.

Reba looked around her by the light of the two lamps, one of which stood on a table. She discovered the missing mattress at once, set up in one corner, together with a couple of blankets. The look she gave Hunter when he joined her was wry.

'Quite a home from home.'

'Welcome to the storm-cellar. My grandfather must have had it built into the hillside for just such occasions as these,' Hunter responded with a grin, hanging the lamp from a hook beside a primitive book-case.

'If you're so sure the building is safe, what are you doing down here?' Reba wanted to know, thinking how cosy it was—how intimate. Even the violence still going on above them seemed a long way away.

'It would be no safer than any house if a tree fell through the roof,' he countered reasonably from over by the makeshift bed, where he hunched over a hold-all. When he rose, he held a shirt in his hands. 'This will have to do until your own things dry. I don't have many clothes with me. You'd better dry yourself on one of the blankets first.'

'While you do what? Stand and watch?'

Hunter tossed her the shirt. 'You're forgetting I've seen you with no clothes on before,' he observed drily, bringing colour to her cheeks. 'However, I am willing to turn my back, providing you're quick.'

'Thank you,' she drawled acidly, but the moment his back was turned she stripped off the sodden clothes, tossing them into a corner before rubbing herself dry on a blanket. The rough texture quickly heated up her blood, but not nearly so much as the shirt did when she pulled it over her head without having to undo the buttons. The shirt was silk, and its the softness had an erotic appeal which was not lost on her.

Nor on Hunter, as he turned from the table where he had been pouring two cups of coffee from a Thermos. 'It looks better on you than it ever did on me,' he observed appreciatively.

'I wouldn't know. I've never seen you in anything other than jeans and T-shirts,' she shot back, rolling up the sleeves which were far too long, aware as she did so that Hunter was taking full advantage of the view of her long tanned legs revealed by the shirt, which ended at mid-thigh. As a covering it was decent, but highly provocative.

'You know something, tiger-eyes, you take far too much at face value. Wearing jeans doesn't mean a man can't afford better. Not even a millionaire would wear a tux to sail a yacht!' he said tersely, and, picking up a box from the shelf, walked over to her. 'Sit down and let me look at those cuts.'

He was right, she had made rash assumptions, but that was because she had been looking at a man, not at a wallet. At the time, she had not been looking for a wealthy man, so it had never occurred to her that she had found one. Disheartened, Reba sat on the mattress, and Hunter stood over her. He cleansed the cut on her forehead first, quite detachedly, as if touching her was nothing special, whereas Reba found that the gentle touch of his fingers sent *frissons* of awareness through her system. It made her very conscious of how little she wore, and how close he was. She could feel the waves of heat coming off him, smell the fragrance of him as he concentrated on what he was doing, and she had to bite down hard on her lip not to reveal her reaction to his closeness.

'It's superficial, nothing more than a scratch. You'll be back in front of the cameras in no time,' Hunter pronounced finally. 'You will be going back to work, I take it, now that you aren't going to be Mrs Eliot Thorson the Third?'

She jumped, glancing up in surprise. 'How did you know?'

In answer he briefly picked up her bare left hand before dropping it back in her lap. She should have known he wouldn't miss the absence of the ring.

Her heart contracted. He had been so sure, and, despite her words, she was here, fiancé-less. 'Are you going to crow?'

'Why should I?' he countered smoothly, irritating her hugely.

'Because you've won,' she bit out thickly.

His eyes met hers briefly, and all the knowledge was there. 'I didn't doubt I would. Did you?'

It hurt, because she had fought so hard to make it different. Yet here she was. Back where she had started, only minus the one thing she wanted most. But thinking about that wouldn't help, and she chose instead to challenge his first statement.

'Who said I was ever going to give up working?'

Hunter knelt down beside her. 'Let me see your legs,' he ordered, tutting when she stretched one out and he saw the scratches. He began to clean them carefully. 'A lot of wealthy men wouldn't want their wives to work. Eliot would be one of those, I think.'

Reba had to swallow to moisten her throat in order to answer him, because one of his hands, steadying her leg, was high up along the back of her thigh, and with the other gently stroking the cotton wool, wonderful things were happening inside her.

'A-And what about you? Would you let your...?' His thumb moved, making her jump, bringing vivid blue eyes up to hers. It was hard to go on in the face of the glow which began in his eyes, but somehow she managed it, however falteringly. 'W-Wife w-work?'

Mouth curving sensually, he abandoned one leg and reached for the other, but that scarcely helped the thudding of her heart. He was playing her like a musical instrument, knowing what he was doing to her, and using that to voice his triumph. 'If it was important to her, yes. The need to work isn't necessarily linked to the need for money, although that is the result. Most of us need to feel useful. We need to stretch ourselves, our minds. Some men climb mountains, others simply have to see a job well done. To know it's helping his fellow man.'

'Others design and build boats,' she added, reminding him of what he had not told her.

Hunter tossed the used cotton wool aside, but didn't release her leg. On the contrary, his hand began a hypnotic caress up and down her calf as he looked at her from beneath hooded lids. 'Do you still hold that against me, tiger-eyes? Criticism from you is a little hard to take, you know. Talking of money, which we weren't, what made you finally decide to ditch dear Cousin El yourself? Were you really worried about what I would say, or did you suddenly realise this way you get pleasure *and* profit?'

Pain seemed to lock itself round her heart at the mocking words, and it didn't help to know that she had brought this on herself. He'd meant to hurt her, and she couldn't bear it. 'Damn you!' she shouted, trying to pull free but failing.

'More tears, tiger-eyes? Who are you kidding? You know what side your bread is buttered on, so don't fool yourself this is true love!' he jeered, and, as his scorn smote her, her temper snapped.

'All right, I won't!' she shot back, and tried to kick his hand away with her free foot. But he saw the move coming and, with the speed of light, yanked the leg he was holding, which flung her on to her back. Before she could gather her scattered wits, he was leaning over her, pinning her down with the weight of his body, one muscular thigh clamping her legs.

Reba found herself unable to move, staring up into a face from which all amusement had vanished. All that was left was the smouldering look in his eyes, and that found an answering heat inside her, taking her breath away.

'We always seem to end up fighting, when it's the last thing I really want to do,' Hunter murmured huskily, brushing away the tendrils of damp hair which clung to her cheeks and brow.

It was so tender, so far from the anger she had just felt, that her will to fight melted away. 'What do you want to do?' she whispered, knowing she was inviting an answer which would lead down only one path.

Blue eyes dropped to her mouth, and her lips were already tingling before his lowered to nuzzle them, sipping at them with brief kisses, as if to sup too long

would plunge them too soon into the intoxicating world
of passion. In between, his words stoked a fire which
had never gone out.

'What do I want to do? I want to lose myself in you.
I want to bury myself so deep inside you that no other
man ever would, or ever could, displace me!' he growled,
and finally took her mouth in a kiss of erotic sensuality
which proclaimed his intention of carrying out his
promise.

Reba's lashes fluttered down as her arms rose to close
about his neck. If only he knew he was already there,
an indelible part of her heart, soul and mind. Her love
made her his, even if he didn't believe in its existence,
and words which spoke of possession, and not love,
could not alter that by one iota. Pride was a bankrupt
economy. She didn't care why he wanted her, only that
she wanted to be here. She could not refuse the only part
of him that she would ever get. Time enough later for
regrets, when she was once more alone.

So she kissed him back with all the generosity of her
love, and felt the shock of surprise which went through
him when her tongue stroked his. Hunter pulled away,
frowning down into her shadowed golden eyes.

'No fight?'

Reba licked her lips, her breathing growing steadily
more erratic. 'I want you too much,' she responded
honestly, giving the only answer he would understand.

Even in the subtle glow of the lamps, it was easy to
see his eyes darken. 'No protestations of love this time?'

'Do we need them?' The words came easily, and meant
nothing. It was what she felt inside which counted.

Hunter shook his head, and his hand lowered to the
buttons of the shirt, slowly opening them, his eyes never
leaving her face and seeing the heat rise in her cheeks.
'Just simple, honest passion? A slaking of mutual

desire?' he queried in an undertone, brushing the silk aside to reveal the taut arousal of her breasts.

Reba shivered sensually, feeling her flesh engorge as his hot gaze grazed her. Her body might reveal her wanting, but it hid the deeper need. He could have the part he wanted, and she would take joy from that, and her heart could pretend it held his for all too brief a time.

There was too much emotion inside her to answer with words. Instead, she shrugged her arms out of the sleeves and reached up to curl her fingers into his hair, holding him while she raised herself to close that small gap and kiss him with instinctive sensuality, wanting to give him pleasure, needing to do it for the sake of her soul. She loved this man, and nothing they did could ever be sordid. She was going to make love to him, whether he knew it or not.

Whatever Hunter was thinking as he responded to her kiss, there was only tenderness in the caressing stroke of his hands on her. She knew he wanted her, feeling the hardness of his arousal through his clothes, but his control was awesome. He moved with exquisite slowness to each new caress, drawing her to the very limits of endurance. Her breasts were aching points of pleasure which he teased with merciless flicks of fingers and tongue, and then abandoned. The torturous path he took across her quivering belly to the dark shadow below had her arching her back in delirium, and when his intimate caress probed on, her thighs parted willingly. She moved against the stroking caress, breath rasping from her throat as he pushed her towards the edge, only to abandon her once again.

When she fell back panting, eyes wild with need for the fulfilment he denied her, Hunter's eyes gleamed with satisfaction. Sitting up, he quickly stripped off his clothes before lying down beside her.

Had she ever doubted his intentions, she knew then that this was to be no revenge. He offered himself openly to her, giving her leave to do to him what he had just done to her, and she accepted gladly. She caressed him tenderly, lovingly, wanting to memorise every inch of him, every shivering groaning response. For Hunter held nothing back, arching as she had done when pleasure took him, eyes glinting, promising delicious tortures when she left him too, craving but unsatisfied.

It was a battle as monumental as the one raging outside, generating a scorching heat as they now came together, slick bodies and tangled limbs reflecting the lamplight as they rolled and fought, inflicting delights which each in turn tried to outdo, until finally victory came from mutual surrender. Heart racing, scarcely able to breathe, she felt Hunter brace himself between her thighs, entering her with a thrust which made her cry out and wrap her legs round him. Then that awesome control failed him, and Reba moved with him to each powerful stroke, clinging on as the tension mounted, coiling inside them until there was nothing else it could do but snap, sending an explosive wave of pleasure through them. As one they both cried out from a feeling so intense it left them shattered and broken upon another shore.

Then came peace.

Reba stirred and sighed deeply, aware of a feeling of such well-being that she didn't want to open her eyes. She felt warm and secure, and knew it came from the strong pair of arms which held her. Hunter lay curved in behind her, his head resting in the hollow of her shoulder and neck. She could hear him breathing, steady and strong, and memory returned.

Reluctantly she blinked her eyes open. The cellar was as it had been, the lamps still burned brightly, but she had no way of knowing if it was dark or light, or how long ago they had fallen into exhausted sleep. The silence struck her then. Had the storm blown itself out, as their own personal one had done? It would be a simple matter to climb the steps and poke her head through the trapdoor and see for herself, but she felt too comfortable to move. Too content.

Not so content that she didn't know that last night had changed nothing. They had shared passion, not love—or so he thought. Had things been different, they might have gone on from here to find a new beginning. She would never know, because now she had to make a demand of him which would forever damn her in his eyes. That hurt unbearably, and unbidden came the question: should she tell him? Lord, she wanted so much to tell him about her mother, but two things held her back.

Harriet Wyeth was a proud woman. She despised pity and hated charity. She had sworn all her children to keep her illness secret, and none of them would ever have dreamed of breaking her trust. Reba had only got permission to tell Eliot because he had been about to become part of the family. Hunter wasn't. Their commitment went no further than the passion they shared, and he paid for. He didn't love her. They had no future. So even if she had permission to tell him, she wouldn't. Telling him wouldn't miraculously make him love her again. Too much had happened. She was proud too. She wouldn't want his pity either.

So this was the best way, the only way. She couldn't even delay it, because there was no time. She had to become once more what he already believed her to be. It was her protection and her curse.

Behind her, Hunter sighed heavily and rolled away from her, taking the warmth with him, leaving her chilled. Symbolic? Perhaps, but it gave her the opportunity to turn and watch him while he slept on. If-onlys were pointless. They were just daydreams. The facts were unchangeable.

'Why so pensive?'

Hunter's husky question startled her, making her realise that he must have been watching her for some time. She wondered what else he might have seen, but then decided it really didn't matter. She sat up, feeling the unaccustomed ache of her body, knowing that when it faded the ache in her heart would feel worse.

'It's tomorrow,' she said flatly, reaching for his shirt because it was closer, and slipping it on.

Propping himself up on his elbow, Hunter ran a finger down her thigh. 'Don't you know tomorrow never comes?'

Her laugh sounded scratchy. 'Oh, it comes, believe me.' Now she turned to look at him, trying to ignore the magnificent picture he made stretched out beside her. 'I believe we also have a bargain.'

Unfazed, Hunter smiled confidently, keeping up that small stroking movement. 'I like the way you do business.'

She slapped his hand away because she wanted it to continue. 'I'm serious, Hunter!'

Her tone got through, and he tipped his head consideringly. 'Hmm, I can see that you are. You seem to have learnt the first rule of business, tiger-eyes. You've lowered my defences, so you'd better tell me what's on your mind.'

Reba swallowed to moisten a suddenly dry mouth. What she had to say sounded so bald that she shuddered to think of it, yet she had to go on. 'You want us to continue as lovers, don't you?'

Now it was Hunter's turn to sit up, bringing him far too close for her comfort. 'After last night, I know you won't be averse to it either.'

He sounded different somehow, warmer than he had done since they had met again. Suddenly she wondered if she was making another big mistake, but there was no time for doubts. All the same, she was shaking, and she had to press her hands together hard to prevent it showing. 'I wouldn't be here if I didn't. However, it appears to me I've kept my side of the bargain. Now it's up to you to keep yours,' she declared huskily.

She could feel the change in him as he tensed. 'Meaning?' he demanded through clenched teeth, and she closed her eyes.

'I think a sign of good faith is in order, don't you?' she enlarged, and, in case he didn't yet understand, made herself add, 'Last night you mentioned profit...'

The word hung between them forever. When at last he spoke, his voice was frosty. 'I see. And just how much profit do you think last night was worth?'

Reba desperately wanted to cry as something curled up and died inside her. Her voice was flat as she stated the exact amount she needed for her mother's operation. Hunter caught his breath sharply, and when she forced herself to look at him it was to see his jaw working furiously as he kept hold of his temper.

When he smiled, it nearly killed her. 'You don't come cheap, do you? Very well, tiger-eyes, I'll write you out a cheque, but be assured, I intend to get my money's worth!'

Hot colour stormed her cheeks, then flooded out, leaving her white. 'A bargain is a bargain.'

As if her words were the last straw, Hunter was on his knees in an instant, catching her by the shoulders and shaking her roughly. 'Damn you, Reba, couldn't you put greed aside for a moment?'

It wasn't greed, it was necessity. 'You made the rules!' she returned, wanting to scream at him but managing to keep her head.

His fingers bit hard into her shoulders but he didn't notice. 'So I did, but stupidly I didn't think you'd follow them quite to the letter!'

'Then you were mistaken, weren't you?' she snapped, gasping when he thrust her away.

'It seems I've been wrong about a lot of things!' he declared in distaste. Standing up, he reached for his clothes, pulling them on with angry movements that made her flinch inwardly. 'You'd better get dressed. I'm going up to check on the damage.'

Reba watched him go, feeling battered. Wearily she went in search of her clothes, still lying tossed in the corner. The raincoat was beyond hope, but her own shorts, top and panties were virtually dry. She dressed quickly, spurred on by her own goading thoughts. Her hair was a mess, and she knew she must look as if she had been dragged through a hedge backwards, but she didn't care. She had done what she had to do, and nothing else seemed to matter right now.

When she climbed up out of the cellar, the world seemed pretty much as she had left it, except that it felt cooler and smelled fresher. It was barely light, but enough to see by. Hunter was out on the veranda, clearing wind-blown debris away with more effort than the task warranted. She hadn't thought he'd heard her arrival, but then he spoke without turning round.

'The track should be OK. The damage here is light. There might be a tree or two down, but you'll be able to get round them safely. It will take me a while to order transport, but that will give you about two hours to be ready to leave.'

He could have been speaking to a stranger, and that hurt. She bit her lip. 'Where are we going?'

He turned then, his expression sardonic. 'Does it matter? I'll be paying for the privilege! Just get yourself back here in two hours.'

Reba raised a hand to her lips to hold back a sob. 'Hunter, please don't be like this,' she pleaded in a broken whisper, but he only laughed humourlessly.

'As you so rightly said, rules are rules. It's my fault for forgetting you only have one god, Mammon. You can be sure I won't make that mistake again.'

It was pointless to attempt to say more. She had made a mess of things, and now she had to live with the consequences. She had a promise of the money, and she had to keep that in mind all the time. It was the only thing which made this situation remotely tolerable.

She simply walked away without looking back, keeping her concentration fully on the track. There were slippery leaves everywhere, and every so often she had to negotiate a fallen palm. When she emerged back at the house, all was quiet, roof and shutters intact. Once the clearing up had been done, there would be nothing to show that the storm had ever happened, but she knew she would always bear the scars. She slipped inside and up to her room unnoticed. She doubted if anyone had even known she had gone. By the time she heard sounds of movement, she had had a long soak in the bath and washed her hair, and her bags stood packed beside the door.

She took them down with her, leaving them by the front door. Good manners meant she must say goodbye, even if she didn't feel like it. When she walked out on to the terrace, the returned servants had already made inroads into the clearing up. Breakfast was ready, the table and chairs set up, and they were making a start on removing the shutters. Pouring herself a cup of coffee, which was all she thought she could stomach right then, Reba wandered over to the parapet, staring out to sea. The water was grey. She felt grey too.

That was where Eliot found her fifteen minutes later. She glanced up at the sound of his footsteps, and stiffened. They were no longer even friends, and she couldn't pretend otherwise.

'Good morning. The house doesn't seem to have suffered any damage,' she said, determined to be civil.

'How would you know? When I went to your room about half-past one this morning, to see how you were, you weren't there,' he commented frostily, and her heart lurched painfully.

'You came to my room?' she repeated faintly, and he nodded.

'Where were you, Reba?'

She had gone through too much already this morning to suffer this catechism mildly. Her good intentions vanished instantly. 'Would it suffice to know I was with Hunter, or do you require a blow-by-blow account?' she returned coldly. He had no right to pass judgement on her. They were no longer engaged.

Eliot's colour rose. 'My God, you're even quite brazen about it!' he exclaimed disgustedly.

Indignation had her eyes flashing gold fire. 'I don't think what I do is any of your business, in the circumstances.'

'You've been carrying on with him behind my back all the time, haven't you?' he charged nastily, making her blood boil.

'I was completely loyal to you while we were engaged but, seeing that we aren't any longer, I'm not ashamed of admitting I already knew Hunter before I agreed to marry you. I didn't know he was your cousin, and I certainly never expected to see him again.'

'What you mean is, if you'd known he had money, you never would have accepted me in the first place,' he accused next. 'Does *he* know you only want him for his money?'

Her eyes felt gritty from unshed tears. 'Yes, but I'm leaving with him all the same. Please say goodbye to your mother for me.' When she would have walked away he caught her arm, turning her so that he could examine her face. What he saw had him laughing aloud.

'Well, well, well! You're in love with him, aren't you?'

Reba could have lied, but the emotion which filled her chest at the question made the option untenable. 'I'll always love him,' she confessed proudly, and jerked herself free.

She was about to go and collect her luggage when the sound of a helicopter approaching took them both by surprise. They looked up in time to see it fly over the island, but quickly lost sight of it, although it could still be heard. She knew it was her transport off the island, and she went and picked up her cases, but when she turned, Eliot blocked her way.

His eyes glittered tauntingly. 'He doesn't love you, though, does he?'

The accurate gibe made her wince. Embattled, she held his gaze. 'No. Does that satisfy your pride?'

He laughed, unpleasant to the last. 'Almost. I think I've already seen my revenge. I hope you'll be very unhappy, Reba. In fact, I'd almost bet on it that you are!'

'Then you'd be wrong. Being with Hunter has always made me happy. There's never been anyone else I wanted to share my life with!'

That wiped his smile away. 'But you agreed to marry me.'

'I had no choice. If you understood the concept of real love, you'd know that!' she responded heatedly, and they faced each other in angry silence.

'Are you ready, Reba?'

Neither of them had heard Hunter arrive, and they both spun round. All the colour left her cheeks as she saw him standing at the top of the steps. How long had he been there? What had he heard? His face was shuttered; there was nothing to be read there.

'Yes,' she acknowledged, brushing past the now silent Eliot. Hunter came forward to take the cases from her. Their eyes met, and his were guarded, remote.

'There's still time to change your mind,' he said coldly, and her stomach lurched. Surely it wouldn't always be like this?

She shook her head. 'No. No, there isn't. Let's go.'

Something flickered in the very depths of his eyes, but was swiftly gone. 'After you,' he said with extreme politeness, and with a heavy heart she stepped off into an uncertain future.

When Hunter had said he'd arrange transport, Reba hadn't visualised being taken to the mainland by helicopter and then transferring to a gleaming Lear jet. Her bruised heart got a little more battered as she noted these trappings of wealth. She felt his eyes on her again. He had been watching her for most of the helicopter flight, and it was beginning to make her feel very nervous. It occurred to her that she should at least say something which was in character.

'Very impressive,' she muttered as they mounted the steps of the jet, to where the pilot waited to greet them.

'Think it's the style you could soon get accustomed to?' Hunter enquired sardonically, and she winced, unable to utter another word.

The moment they were aboard, the steps were removed and the door shut. The pilot exchanged words with Hunter, then nodded politely and headed for the cockpit, while a smiling stewardess indicated the seat she should take. She collapsed into it, allowed herself to be strapped in, and within seconds the jet was thundering down the runway and they were airborne.

Reba took her eyes from the window to discover that she was under surveillance again. Edgily she glanced away. What was he trying to do, shrivel her up? Her eyes went to her wrist, wondering how long the flight would be, but she had left the diamond watch behind, and rubbed her bare wrist self-consciously.

'Lose your watch?' Hunter queried dulcetly. 'I'll have to buy you another.'

That brought her head up. 'You will not! I have a perfectly good watch in my case.'

One eyebrow lifted, 'It would please me to give you things,' he pointed out.

'And it would please me to throw them back at you!' she retorted fiercely, before realising that that was hardly in character at all. 'I mean...' She swallowed hard and hesitated, noting the gleam in his eyes.

'Yes, what do you mean, tiger-eyes?' he prompted instantly, making it impossible to go on.

'Nothing. Leave me alone, Hunter. I'm tired.'

'You should be,' he responded obliquely, and, the seatbelt sign going off at that moment, got to his feet. 'I'm going to change. Make yourself at home. Beth will get you anything you want.'

Reba watched him disappear through a door and sank back miserably into the comfortable seat. This was worse than she had imagined. Hunter was behaving very oddly, and she... She was making a hash of everything!

'Can I get you something to drink?' The stewardess's enquiry made her jump, and she was just about to ask for a stiff brandy when she caught sight of the man who re-entered the cabin.

'What's your preference, Reba?' Hunter asked sardonically—a vastly different Hunter in silk shirt and tie, handmade shoes, and the trousers of what must surely be an expensive Italian suit. When she remained silent, his lips quirked. 'Thank you, Beth, we'll both have brandy.' Having dismissed the young woman, he sat down opposite Reba, crossing his legs casually, regarding her with mocking amusement.

'Do you approve?' he taunted, taking the two glasses the returning stewardess held out.

Reba took the drink he proffered, catching the flash of gold cuff-links, and recognising the gold Rolex on his wrist. 'You look...different.' A stranger. Handsome, but not the man she knew. It was as if the donning of expensive clothes had put a barrier between them— keeping them apart. She knew it was deliberate, and took a sip of the fiery liquid out of sheer desperation, but although it burned, she remained frozen inside.

His eyes laughed at her over the top of his glass as he took an appreciative mouthful of the brandy. 'How else would you expect the owner of Backbay Marine to look, tiger-eyes?'

She raised a trembling hand to rub a sudden throbbing in her temple. 'Why?'

Those blue eyes didn't waver from hers. 'I thought you would like proof that I really can afford you,' he revealed, daring her to respond.

'I never doubted it. Eliot said it was the best.'

He smiled at that. 'It is. It earns me a very great deal of money. So you really can have anything you want.'

Anything? I want your love, was the cry from her heart, and that's the one thing you won't ever give me now!

'Well?'

Was he waiting for a list? Reba glanced down at the brandy she still held, and set the glass aside with a grimace of distaste. 'I don't want anything.'

Hunter looked doubtful. 'No? What about a mink coat, or a Porsche? I could probably buy you a condo somewhere, but it would have to be convenient. I wouldn't want to travel far every time I needed to see you. You'll have to tell me which designers you prefer, so that I can open up accounts for you. Have I missed anything?' he challenged bitingly.

Reba wondered if there was ever to be an end to the misery they could bring each other. He was cutting her pride to shreds, and hot tears burned the backs of her eyes. 'Damn you, shut up!' she cried, driven to the end of her rope, and not caring who heard.

'In a minute. You're forgetting this.' His hand slid into his trouser pocket and drew out a cheque-book and pen. He flipped open the cover, and she watched as he filled out the necessary details, signing the cheque with a flourish before tearing it out and offering it to her.

She stared at it as if it were about to jump up and bite her, and it was incredibly hard to reach out and take it. To find he did not immediately release it brought her darkened gaze to his. What now? What further refinement was he thinking of?

'You know, this is rather an odd amount to ask for. In fact, it sounds more like an exact amount. Care to comment on that?' he asked mildly.

Her stomach lurched, and she knew that her eyes widened anxiously. 'No,' she refused huskily.

His eyebrows rose. 'Just the first number which came into your head?'

She was reduced to monosyllables. 'Yes.'

Finally he released the cheque. 'Interesting.' He rose to his feet and stretched. They might have been discussing the weather, for all the concern he showed. 'Enjoy the rest of the flight. We should be landing in an hour.'

Reba didn't relax the tight control she had on herself until she heard the cockpit door close behind him. Then her breath left her on a shaky sigh which was half a sob, and she let her head fall back against the seat. Tears scorched the backs of her eyes, and she pressed a hand to her lips to hold back another threatening sob. It wouldn't help to cry. Nothing could ease the pain inside. It was incredible to believe that, although they had loved each other so much, a few careless words had brought them to this.

She wanted to go to him and say, Listen to me, I can explain. But he wouldn't believe her. How could he, after all that had been said and done? Wouldn't he just laugh if she swore she loved him? Wouldn't he just die if she begged him to love her again the way he had before? She wanted to do it, and if she had been free to do so she might have risked his scorn and tried it anyway, because she really had little pride left. If there were just the faintest chance, she might take it—if she were free. But she wasn't. Too much depended on her, and that would stop her every time.

A single tear tracked a path down her cheek, but she didn't have the strength to brush it away.

CHAPTER TEN

ON THE following Friday Reba got an unexpected telephone call. She had parted from Hunter at the airport at the beginning of the week, and hadn't heard anything from him since. He had said he would ring her, but since then, nothing. She didn't know what to make of it. However much she might dislike the situation, she was prepared to keep her side of the bargain, and the days of waiting were doing her no good whatsoever.

So when the telephone rang that morning, she was fully expecting to hear his voice at the other end of the line. It turned out, however, to belong to someone employed at her bank. The message it delivered stunned her so much that it didn't sink in, and she had to ask for it to be repeated.

'I'm afraid I have to tell you the cheque you recently deposited with us has been cancelled. The money cannot be credited to your account. As the amount was quite large, we thought it best to advise you immediately so that you can take any necessary action,' the voice obligingly repeated, not knowing what a blow it was delivering.

Reba knew, and her blood ran cold. 'Thank you,' she said, automatically polite, returning the receiver to its rest, while the enormity of what she had heard expanded to fill her. As it did so, shock turned to anger.

Hunter had cancelled the cheque! She couldn't believe it, and yet she knew it was true. Why, dammit? Why? Why? Why? God, after all she had had to go through, how dared he do this to her! It had to be revenge. He had changed his mind, but instead of telling her immediately, he had deceived her. Lulled her into a false sense of security out of a simple lust for revenge! No wonder she hadn't heard from him! He knew she would get the message very soon!

Her hands balled into impotent fists, nails scoring into her palms as she digested the niceties of his plan. Her anger boiled over at the sense of betrayal. She hadn't thought him capable of such a thing. It was murder, cold-blooded murder, and she was damned if she would let him get away with it.

Coldly furious, she grabbed up the telephone and spent the next few minutes trying to find a telephone number for him. Finally she was given the number of Backbay Marine, and her fingers jabbed it out. As soon as the ringing was answered, she barked out her request.

'I want to speak to Hunter Jamieson.'

'I'm sorry, but Mr Jamieson is not here today,' a polite female voice replied.

'Damn!' Reba bit her lip hard at the disappointment. 'Do you know where he is? Can I reach him somewhere?'

'I'm afraid I can't say. Shall I take your name and ask him to call you?'

Reba knew she was being given a polite brush-off and wasn't prepared to accept it. 'Listen, this is a matter of life and death. I *have* to contact him immediately!' she declared forcefully, knowing it wasn't a lie, and might very well be more true than she cared to think about.

The voice at the other end hesitated. 'Well, if it's an emergency...?'

'Of course it's an emergency. I wouldn't be ringing otherwise, would I?' Reba shot back with heavy irony, hoping the other woman wouldn't call that into question.

Fortunately she didn't. 'I have an address, but no telephone number. I can try to find one if you'd care to wait.'

'No, no, just the address will do,' she said quickly, and jotted it down hurriedly. With a brief word of thanks, she slammed the receiver down and stared at the piece of paper. Just you wait, Hunter Jamieson. Just you wait, she promised, and dashed off to change.

The address was that of an advertising agency. Reba took the elevator to the fifteenth floor a little before ten-thirty. She had taken the time to put on make-up, and was glad she had chosen to wear cream trousers and a navy silk blouse, for the receptionist who greeted her with a friendly smile, was immaculately turned out.

'You're Reba Wyeth—I recognised you instantly. But I don't think you have an appointment with us today, do you?' Concern that she might have made a mistake was mixed with polite enquiry as she studied the appointment diary in front of her.

'I don't have an appointment, but I have come to see Hunter Jamieson. I was told he was here,' Reba explained in a tight voice, nails beating out a rapid tattoo on the desk-top.

The receptionist looked justifiably confused. 'Why, yes, he is here. Down in the board-room.' She pointed along a carpeted corridor, and Reba needed no further encouragement. She headed in that direction, followed by the cries of the receptionist trying to call her back.

She didn't bother to knock on the door, and was about to walk right in when it opened ahead of her, revealing a smiling young man who very nearly bumped into her. 'Thanks,' she flung at him as she brushed past into the room.

The man's smile turned to a frown as he followed her. 'Can I help you?' he demanded sternly, trying to get ahead of her to stop her.

Reba didn't spare him a glance; her mind was set on another quarry. 'No. I'm looking for——'

'Me,' Hunter supplied, moving out from where the open door had been shielding him from her. 'It's OK, Sandy, I'll deal with Miss Wyeth.'

Sandy glanced round, obviously recognising the name. His antennae told him this was something he would be well out of. 'OK, Hunter, you know where to find me if you need me,' he conceded, and departed in good order, but not without a backward glance of keen curiosity.

Hunter shut the door behind him, locking it and pocketing the key. He looked perfectly relaxed as he leant back against the wood, hands in pockets and feet crossed at the ankles.

'To what do I owe the pleasure of this visit?' he queried mildly, bringing angry colour to Reba's pale cheeks.

'Don't play with me! You know damn well why I'm here! Damn you, Hunter, I could kill you for what you've done!' she cried furiously.

Smiling faintly, he studied the tip of one highly polished shoe. 'Ah, you know about the cheque.'

The fact he didn't deny it took her aback, and her throat tightened. 'They rang me this morning. Dear God, do you hate me so much that you could do such a thing?' she cried, feeling anger being swamped by other, more painful, emotions. Suddenly she was on the verge of tears.

Hunter crossed his arms and studied her carefully. 'If I hated you, tiger-eyes, I would have let you cash the cheque,' he said softly, taking her breath away.

Reba blinked, staring at him hard. That made no sense. 'What do you mean?' she demanded, the feeling growing that, in the space of a few minutes, this meeting had got away from her.

'I mean you're making an awful lot of fuss about a cheque given to you for... services rendered,' Hunter replied easily, bringing shamed colour to her cheeks at his choice of words.

It was enough to have her forgetting caution. 'So would you if you needed the money!' she snarled back, then gasped as she realised what she had said. Oh God! 'Open that door and let me out!' she ordered immediately, desperately needing to retreat and regroup her forces.

Hunter shook his head. 'What do you need the money for, Reba?'

Her jaw set. 'None of your business. Let me out!'

Unimpressed, he fixed her with a gimlet eye. 'Not until you tell me what you needed it for.'

Crossing her arms defiantly, Reba refused to look at him. 'I lied.'

'Then you aren't interested in a proposition I have to make?'

'Another proposition? Boy, you don't give up, do you?' she jeered, and stormed away to the window, staring sightlessly at the traffic crawling down below.

'You've not heard this one before.'

'I don't want to hear it now,' she retorted, then jumped in surprise as his hand swung her round. She hadn't heard him move, but he was now right beside her.

'You're going to hear it anyway,' he decided, supremely in control.

She raised a mocking eyebrow. 'Really? Well, the answer is no, so you can save your breath to cool your porridge.'

Hunter drew in a deep breath, eyes flashing a warning it would be as well for her to heed. 'You know, it would give me a great deal of satisfaction to put you over my knee and whale the tar out of you!'

'Lay one finger on me and I'll have you charged with assault!'

Hunter smiled, then reached out one finger, placed it against the centre of her chest and pushed. 'Shut up and sit down, Reba. You should never refuse a deal until you know what's on offer.'

She slapped his hand away, going to the chair only because it put some distance between them. 'All right, I'm listening,' she declared, finally sitting down.

Hunter came round to perch on the corner of the desk, one leg swinging free. From the inside pocket of his jacket, he produced two pieces of paper. 'I have here a cheque for a million dollars and a marriage licence. You can have the money, but only if you marry me.'

Shock had followed upon shock so rapidly recently that she hadn't thought it possible to feel more, but this shattered her composure totally, and she trembled in reaction. 'What?'

There was the faintest curve to the corner of his mouth, but his blue eyes were shuttered. 'You heard me. I'm giving you everything your gold-digging little heart desires. Say you'll marry me, and all I have to do is pick up the phone and an account will be opened in your name. All that money will be yours to do with as you wish, no questions asked,' he informed her calmly, and Reba gasped.

A million dollars? It was practically everybody's dream, and yet she hated the very mention of it. For it told her just what he thought of her. She didn't want his money, she wanted his love. He was offering her everything but that and, although her need was desperate, she couldn't take it. Not from him. She loved him too much to do it. If she accepted, he would always think it was because of the money, and he'd never believe she loved him. And, when the passion faded, all that would be left was his contempt. She just couldn't do it.

That brought her head up. Standing on very shaky legs, she crossed over to him and held out her hand. 'Give me the cheque,' she ordered hoarsely, and when, after the briefest hesitation, he handed it to her, she quickly tore it into tiny pieces and flung them in his face. 'I don't want a million dollars, and I won't marry you. All I want is what I asked for. Are you going to give it to me?' she challenged as firmly as she could.

Hunter's face was shuttered once more. Reaching into his pocket, he took out the key as he stood up. 'No, I'm not,' he refused calmly.

Shaken, Reba pressed her lips together to stop their trembling. 'Then damn you, Hunter!' she cursed, and made a grab for the key.

Unfortunately he was quicker than she, closing his fingers around it and catching hold of her wrist in a vice-like grip. 'You're going nowhere unless it's with me, tiger-eyes,' he commanded, pulling her after him towards the door.

'Let me go!' she shouted, as he unlocked the barrier and flung it wide.

'Never!' Hunter retorted grimly, towing her along in his wake as he headed for the lift.

As he punched the button, she flashed him a glare and tried to prise his fingers loose, but they stuck like glue. 'I don't ever want to see you again! Do you hear me? Not ever!' she cried passionately, uncaring of the gaping faces which stared after them.

The lift arrived and he hauled her in with him, quickly hitting the garage button. 'Tough. You're stuck with me, sweets. At least for another couple of hours. After that, we'll see if you've changed your mind,' he informed her tersely, bundling her struggling form out into the virtually deserted garage level, where a chauffeur nimbly climbed from a limousine to hold open the rear door while Hunter pushed her inside. Then the door was shut behind them, and only when the driver was back in his seat, and the central locking in force, did he let her go.

Hugging the corner of the seat, Reba rubbed her maltreated wrist. 'I hate you!'

Hunter crossed his legs and sent her a mocking glance. 'I hate you too.'

His indifference took the wind out of her sails, leaving her crumpled up with her own misery. How had she been brought to this? Where was he taking her? Nothing was going the way it should have done, and she no longer knew what was going on. If it had been anyone else but Hunter, she would have been frightened, but fear had no place in the seething cauldron of emotions which brewed inside her.

'Where are you taking me?'

His lips twitched. 'For a ride in the country. My treat.'

'I don't accept treats from two-faced Indian-givers!' Reba snapped back instantly.

'Well, I don't enjoy giving them to liars, tiger-eyes,' he responded.

'I didn't lie!' she gasped.

'Not much!' Hunter snorted.

'We had a deal!' she reminded him sickly, heart thudding wildly in her chest.

Hunter laughed. 'We had a hell of a lot more than that!' he said meaningfully, holding her golden eyes with his blue ones until hers were forced to drop.

'I don't know what you're talking about,' she told him, shifting uneasily in her seat. She had the distinct feeling that the ground had just been swept out from under her, but she still couldn't see the hole.

His teeth flashed as he grinned briefly. 'Selective ignorance isn't going to save you. You're running up one hell of a bill. You'd better start thinking how you intend to pay it.'

She refused to understand, knowing she was already on very shaky ground. He was talking in riddles, and she didn't know if she dared try to work them out, for fear of reading into them something which wasn't there. In an attempt to ignore him, she stared fixedly out of the window, and that was how, an hour later, she first saw the building they were making for.

Reba sat up straighter as they sped through the entrance, the sign printed on her brain. 'This is the Chamberlain Hospital,' she pronounced faintly, turning troubled eyes on her silent companion. 'What are we doing here?'

'Visiting,' he informed her drily as the car drew to a halt before the entrance. 'Are you going to behave, or will I have to send for restraints?'

She was too numbed by shock to fight. 'I'll behave,' she promised, while her brain began to work overtime. Why this hospital? Why the very one her mother would have been booked into if only Hunter had kept his part of the bargain? Could it be sheer coincidence, or...? What did it all mean? Docilely she followed him into the antiseptic precincts, acknowledging that he seemed to know his way about.

'Is it a relative of yours we're visiting?' Reba asked as they proceeded up to the top floor.

Hunter led the way along a corridor until he stopped before one room. 'I certainly look upon her as a relative,' he confirmed, holding open the door for her to precede him inside. 'After you,' he said politely, and with a wary look she stepped inside.

The closing of the door behind her went unnoticed as she stared dumbfounded at the woman in the bed. 'Mum!'

Harriet Wyeth glanced up from the magazine she was reading and held out her arms, smiling as her daughter rushed into them. 'Reba! I wasn't expecting you until later.'

After assuring herself that her mother was real and not a figment of her imagination, Reba pushed herself free, wiping away emotional tears as she stared at the very last person she had expected to see. 'I wasn't expecting you at all! What are you doing here? How did you get here? Where's Maggie?' The questions flowed off her tongue, making Harriet laugh.

'Silly, you know what I'm doing here. As for how, Hunter arranged it all. He flew over to get me in his own plane two days ago. He brought his cousin Lucy with him, and she's staying with Maggie and Christopher until after the operation.'

Reba felt peculiarly light-headed. 'Hunter arranged it?' she queried faintly, automatically looking around for him, but finding that he hadn't joined her in the room. 'Mum, I don't understand!'

Harriet patted her hand. 'Of course not. It's a surprise. He told me how you had asked him to handle the financial side of things, but as he knew how hard you had had to work to raise the money, he thought it would be a nice surprise to bring me over himself and relieve you of any more worry. After all, he is almost family.'

Reba wondered if she might have gone mad without realising it. 'Family?' she parroted, while all she could think of was that Hunter knew. He knew everything. And if her mother was here, then that could only mean he had arranged for the money to be paid. Which meant all this had happened before she went to see him today. So what had that confrontation in the board-room been all about?

Into all these chaotic thoughts, her mother's soothing voice penetrated like a lancet. 'Well, you are going to marry him, so that makes him family. I'm so pleased. I really like him, darling. He told me how worried you were and that he wanted to take the burden off your shoulders, and of course I couldn't argue with that. I could see that he loves you very much.'

Only one sentence really got through, and Reba felt her colour come and go. 'Hunter told you we were going to be married?'

Harriet laughed reminiscently. 'He had to introduce himself, darling. How else could I believe who he was? He told me he was Eliot's cousin, and that you broke off your engagement because the pair of you took one look at each other and fell in love. So romantic!'

Reba hardly knew what to think. 'Hunter said all that, and you believed him?'

Her mother's smile faded slowly. 'Shouldn't I have done? Isn't it true? Don't you love him?'

Seeing the change her careless words had wrought, Reba could only speak the truth. 'Oh, yes, I love him, Mum,' she admitted, although she couldn't go on and confirm the marriage.

Mrs Wyeth didn't think it necessary. 'Well, that's all right then. Maggie would have been most upset. She's looking forward to being your bridesmaid.'

It was like drowning, Reba decided. She felt helpless in the pull of a current stronger than herself. Either Hunter was acting some monstrous lie, or he meant every word of it. She couldn't believe he would do the former, and yet the latter seemed even more incredible. It would be a miracle if he really loved her, and yet a small voice which wouldn't be ignored asked why he would have done it if he didn't.

Lord, she wanted to believe, but how could she, after all she had done? Yet nothing else made any sense.

For the rest of the visit she was only half concentrating on what her mother said, and when she finally said she had to go, promising to return later, her thoughts were already leaping ahead to her meeting with Hunter.

He wasn't in the corridor, and she went in search of him with a fast-beating heart. However, he wasn't in the building, and when she got to where the limousine was parked, she discovered that he wasn't there either. It was the chauffeur who filled in the blanks.

'Mr Jamieson left, miss.'

'Left?' It was the very last thing she was expecting, and it stunned her.

'Yes, miss. He had the helicopter come and collect him. But he left you a message.'

Her heart sank. She had a dreadful feeling that she knew what it was going to say. 'OK, give it to me,' she said, squaring her shoulders.

'He said to tell you if you wanted to see him, you'd know where to find him. If not, I was to take you back to town.'

Reba's heart took off at a gallop. She had been expecting to hear goodbye, but this was something different. But what did he mean, she would know where to find him? She didn't know where he lived, for heaven's sake! Except the island, and he surely couldn't mean there. Or the yacht. Yacht? Inspiration made her gasp.

She turned to the waiting chauffeur. 'Do you know a place called Backbay Marine?'

'The company? It's down the coast, miss.'

Bingo. Reba opened the front passenger door and prepared to climb in. 'Take me there, please.'

The chauffeur came to attention. 'Yes, miss, but it will take some considerable time,' he warned.

Reba smiled. 'I don't care how long it takes, just so long as I get there,' she said, knowing she was going to the right place, and hoping against hope that she knew how it was all going to end.

She had had the chauffeur drop her off outside the office of the boatyard. It was deserted, the drive having taken them beyond working hours, but she could hear the sound of hammering, so she knew that someone was about. It was a beautiful evening, still very hot, but there was a refreshing breeze coming off the river. She followed the curve of it as she made for the sound, and, as she rounded the side of a building, she saw Hunter perched on top of a ladder, nailing new shingles on the roof of a shed. He had changed clothes, and looked more like the man she remembered, dressed solely in cut-offs, the rest of his quite magnificent body glistening in the sun.

She had thought her arrival had gone unnoticed, but Hunter must have heard her approach, for as she stopped beneath him he ceased hammering and looked down at her.

'What took you so long?' he mocked, but there was a light in his eyes which set her heart tripping.

She let her bag drop to the ground, and put her hands on her hips. 'I don't keep a helicopter in my handbag!'

'Well, now, that means you're either going to have to save up all your pennies and buy your own, or marry a man who already has one,' Hunter declared as he descended agilely to the ground and stood before her.

'According to my mother, I'm already going to. Unless you lied,' she challenged, and then caught her breath as he reached out a finger to wipe away the drip of perspiration which was trailing a path down towards the valley between her breasts.

'I wouldn't lie to your mother,' he murmured, licking the salty moisture from his finger, yet never taking his blue gaze from hers. Her stomach tightened on a painful wave of desire.

'Didn't you think of asking me first?'

'Nope. You're going to marry me, tiger-eyes, make no mistake about that. Fancy a beer?'

Bemused, she nodded, and climbed up on to the porch while he disappeared inside the shed. He returned with two misted bottles. Tossing one over to her, he propped himself on the rail and took a long swallow. She found herself following the movement of his throat with sensual pleasure, and forgot to breathe.

'So, you found me. Have much trouble?'

Jolted back to awareness, Reba rolled the bottle between her hands, suddenly nervous now that she was here facing him. A glance at his face showed that he had been aware of her watching him, and had enjoyed it as much as she had. That openly sensual acknowledgement made her tremble, but not from fear. It was hard to frame intelligent thought.

'Not when I thought about it. But why did you go? You must have known I'd want to speak to you.'

Hunter uttered a soft laugh. 'Because I was human enough to want *you* to come after *me*. And here you are.'

'Yes, here I am,' Reba agreed softly.

He took another mouthful of beer. 'How is your mother?'

Reba raised a diffident shoulder. 'She's fine. She——' She broke off abruptly, dragging a hand through her hair. 'Hunter, this is ridiculous! Why didn't you tell me what you'd done, instead of staging that charade in the board-room?'

'I was going to. In the board-room, when you told me why you needed the money,' he returned levelly, quirking an eyebrow and bringing colour to her cheeks.

'But... But you already knew why,' Reba protested.

A nerve jerked in his jaw. 'Hard as it may be to believe, tiger-eyes, I had this burning need to have you trust me enough to tell me yourself!' he said tightly, and she gained some idea then how her silence must have hurt him.

'You don't understand. It wasn't my secret to tell.' She pressed trembling lips together. 'I do trust you, Hunter. I always have.'

His head went back, breath exploding from him in a sigh. 'You have a hell of a way of showing it!'

She swallowed back painful tears. 'My mother is a proud woman. I couldn't break her trust. I'm sorry. I had no choice.'

Hunter looked at her then, blue eyes softening wryly. 'No. You had no choice. It was thinking that you had which sent me into hell, and hearing that you hadn't which brought me out again.'

The admission made her start. 'I don't understand,' she whispered.

Hunter set his unfinished beer aside and did the same with hers. Then he cupped her face in his hands. 'You told Eliot you had no choice but to agree to marry him. That was when I stopped being angry and started doing some thinking—something which, at the time, you very cleverly made sure I wouldn't do. Why had you had no choice? I asked myself. Because you believed Eliot had the one thing I didn't have—money. Yet, right up until that last day, money wasn't important to you. I'd been around women who only wanted me for my money long enough to tell the difference. When you claimed to be a gold-digger, my emotions got in the way of clear thinking. I couldn't believe I could have been so wrong about you.

'Then I overheard you and Eliot, and I began to wonder if I hadn't been right all the time. I got the idea that perhaps you didn't want money so much as need it. I remembered things you'd told me, like that your mother had been ill. It took me umpteen telephone calls and several hellish days to figure out just what was going on, but I know now, and I'm not likely to forget it in a hurry.'

Her hands rose to cover his, her faint smile coming and going. 'And what did you figure out?'

Briefly his lips came down and brushed over hers. 'Firstly, that I loved you, and always had. Secondly, that if I ever had cause to do something which could hurt you, then I'd do my very best to make you hate me, and spare you the pain.'

So he really did know. Her eyes became molten at the memory. 'Please believe me, I didn't want to do it, but it seemed the only way.'

His forehead came to rest on hers, and his eyes closed. 'You should have told me, Reba,' he growled, and she heard the pain, and her hand went to his nape in an attempt to ease his stress.

'I wanted to. Oh, how I wanted to! But how could I, when I didn't think you could help? Everything went wrong so quickly. Mum got worse. It had to be now or never. I couldn't let her die, so it had to be you I gave up.' It was impossible to hide her own despair, and Hunter groaned in understanding as a sob escaped her.

'Don't cry, tiger-eyes, that tears me apart. I was no help to you, was I? I should have told you who I was in the beginning. This need never have happened if I hadn't been so paranoid about wanting to be loved for myself and not my money.'

After all the mistakes, she wouldn't have him blaming himself. 'We were both vulnerable, but it's over now, thanks to you,' she whispered.

'Your mother will have the operation she needs, and you and I will have each other. That's the important thing,' he responded gruffly.

'Thank you for not telling her where the money came from. I was so worried that if she knew she would refuse to accept it.'

Hunter laughed wryly. 'I'd figured that out. You're not your mother's daughter for nothing. She should be proud of you.'

'I don't know. I'm not proud of a lot of the things I've done. I made such a mess of it. But I do love you, Hunter. Not because of the money, or anything else. I love you because I can't help myself. It's always been you. Only you.'

Hunter kissed her then, taking the love from her lips and giving it back with a depth of passion which rocked them where they stood. His hands strained her to him, and she could feel the tremors go through his body as the tension which they had lived under for so long finally gave way. When he released her enough to look down at her, she found herself gazing deeply into eyes which were no longer shuttered. It was all there for her to see, and she felt emotion threaten to overwhelm her. She was home—really home at last!

Are your lips succulent, impetuous, delicious or racy?

Find out in a very special Valentine's Day promotion—THAT SPECIAL KISS!

Inside four special Harlequin and Silhouette February books are details for THAT SPECIAL KISS! explaining how you can have your lip prints read by a romance expert.

Look for details in the following series books, written by four of Harlequin and Silhouette readers' favorite authors:

Silhouette Intimate Moments #691
Mackenzie's Pleasure by *New York Times* bestselling author Linda Howard

Harlequin Romance #3395
Because of the Baby by Debbie Macomber

Silhouette Desire #979
Megan's Marriage by Annette Broadrick

Harlequin Presents #1793
The One and Only by Carole Mortimer

Fun, romance, four top-selling authors, plus a **FREE** gift! This is a very special Valentine's Day you won't want to miss! Only from Harlequin and Silhouette.

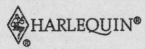

VAL96

Take 4 bestselling love stories FREE
Plus get a FREE surprise gift!

Special Limited-time Offer

Mail to Harlequin Reader Service®

3010 Walden Avenue
P.O. Box 1867
Buffalo, N.Y. 14269-1867

YES! Please send me 4 free Harlequin Presents® novels and my free surprise gift. Then send me 6 brand-new novels every month, which I will receive months before they appear in bookstores. Bill me at the low price of $2.66 each plus 25¢ delivery and applicable sales tax, if any*. That's the complete price and a savings of over 10% off the cover prices—quite a bargain! I understand that accepting the books and gift places me under no obligation ever to buy any books. I can always return a shipment and cancel at any time. Even if I never buy another book from Harlequin, the 4 free books and the surprise gift are mine to keep forever.

106 BPA AW6U

Name	(PLEASE PRINT)	
Address	Apt. No.	
City	State	Zip

This offer is limited to one order per household and not valid to present Harlequin Presents® subscribers. *Terms and prices are subject to change without notice. Sales tax applicable in N.Y.

UPRES-995

You're About to Become a *Privileged Woman*

Reap the rewards of fabulous free gifts and benefits with proofs-of-purchase from Harlequin and Silhouette books

Pages & Privileges™

It's our way of thanking you for buying our books at your favorite retail stores.

PROOF OF PURCHASE
HP-PP95
Offer expires October 31, 1996

Harlequin and Silhouette—
the most privileged readers in the world!

For more information about Harlequin and Silhouette's PAGES & PRIVILEGES program call the Pages & Privileges Benefits Desk: 1-503-794-2499

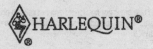

HARLEQUIN®

HP-PP95